THE SISTER'S TWIN

An absolutely gripping mystery thriller
that will take your breath away

JANE ADAMS

Ray Flowers Book 4

JOFFE
BOOKS

Joffe Books, London
www.joffebooks.com

First published in Great Britain in 2021

Cover art by Dee Dee Book Covers

ISBN: 978-1-78931-727-5

PROLOGUE

Five years earlier

Sometimes, all it takes is the final piece, the last section of the puzzle and everything else in your life begins to make sense. It had been that way when he first saw the Book of Angels, the day the woman at the psychic fair had read his fortune in the cards. The woman had been young, a little too heavily made-up for his taste and dressed in what he thought of as hippie clothes. He had been to a number of these events — he had always been curious about motivations, always eager to examine human beings in their many and varied manifestations.

'You have the Angel of Transformations. That's similar to the Death card in the standard tarot,' she had told him, and then, as though suddenly conscious of his age and not wanting to give offence, added, 'but please don't worry or be afraid of it. This card means a change is coming to your life, something wonderful and all-embracing. And see, here, the Angel of Justice, the card of correction or resurrection. It means that you have a decision to make, something deep and important to put right. A decision that will set you on a new path where there will be no more regrets, no turning back or turning away. The tide will take you and the oceans of life will be yours to travel.'

He had thought her a charlatan. Most 'readers' at these places were exactly that — no more, no less — though he had found that, on occasion, even those without the skill to see could cast light on his shadow. But her words had struck a chord and the cards had filled him with wonder. The designs were simple and beautiful and loaded with the kind of symbolism that spoke directly to his soul in a way that the tarot had failed to do before.

He had found a stall selling cards and crystals and had bought his own pack of the Book of Angels and the guidebook to go with it. Not just a book of basic interpretation, but a guidebook for the soul, filled with meditations and questions. He had begun to work with it that very night. A certainty had come to him that he should act, that those who had wronged him should be punished, that his unwitting so-called retirement should be ended.

Since then, not a day had passed when he had not read the message in the cards and lived his life according to their meanings. It did not matter to him that most who saw the book may have read a different message or been appalled at the interpretations that he drew from the peaceful meditations. He found what he needed to complete the picture, the pattern of his life. What was needed now was for him to go forward and complete his own spiritual journey. Become, once again, the best that he could be.

The irony was that the charlatan who had read for him had been correct. She had seen death and she had seen the final judgement from which there could be no return. And that death was now, simple and clean, a knife plunged deep into the chest while the woman he had chosen to be first lay sleeping. Her body jerked and stiffened for a moment, but she did not even open her eyes, drifting straight from sleep into death.

He spread the cards across the bed, reading her past and his own future by the dim light of the risen moon, and then he chose a card for her, folded it once and slipped it into her outstretched hand.

CHAPTER 1

Flowers-Mahoney Security did not take on private investigations, as a general rule. It was concerned with the installation and maintenance of security systems, and its occasional tendency to re-examine old or unusual cases that the local police had no interest in pursuing was not something the firm advertised. It was therefore with some surprise that Ray received a visit from an elderly lady who asked him if he was the private eye she had heard about.

Lily Spencer — Miss, as she introduced herself — could have been any age from sixty upward. She was neatly dressed in a suit of royal blue over a plain cream blouse, and her white hair, thick and well cared for, was cut into a stylish bob.

Her make-up was careful and restrained, an eye shadow that defined the shape of her eyes and avoided creasing in the slight wrinkles of her lids, and a touch of lipstick in a coral shade that Ray was certain he recalled his mother's aunt wearing. She seated herself in front of Ray's large desk and composed herself carefully, resting her leather handbag across her knees before speaking. She had a way of lifting her chin that was feisty, even defiant, as though she expected Ray to be trouble and she wanted to be prepared.

She came straight to the point. 'I want you to investigate a murder.'

'A murder?' Ray hadn't been expecting that. 'Have you spoken to the police?'

'Of course I have,' she told him. 'My *first* thought was to go to the police, but would they listen? No. They sent me away without so much as taking down my statement and I didn't know where to turn. Then a young man at the reception directed me to you. He said you used to be a policeman and that you weren't put off by the unusual.'

'I see,' Ray said. He could well imagine any number of his previous colleagues delighting in throwing him a curveball like this. 'Perhaps you should fill me in on the details,' he said in a more conciliatory tone. 'Who is it that was murdered, Miss Spencer? And can you tell me why the police sent you away? It seems a strange thing for them to have done.'

Lily Spencer looked a little uncomfortable but she lifted that determined chin and fixed Ray with her pale blue gaze. 'It's my sister, Rose. Only she's not dead yet. That's the trouble, you see, we have to stop it happening.'

'Has someone threatened her? Miss Spencer, if someone has been issuing threats, then you must tell the police . . .'

But Lily Spencer was shaking her head. 'No, Mr Flowers, it's nothing as simple as that, and I'm afraid that you won't understand any more than your old colleagues did. It's Elspeth. She saw it in the cards, you see, that Rose was going to be killed, and Elspeth is never wrong.'

* * *

The old man had set things in motion but the devil of it was that age and strength had let him down. His own Constraining Angel, just like the one in the cards, had bound and exasperated him. After that one glorious night five years before, his retirement had resumed, unwelcome and frustrating. He looked back now through his book of cuttings and memories, reliving, in the dead of night, past glories, moments when the hunger had been assuaged and he had felt at peace with the world. One vital thing now kept him from despair. Two years ago, someone had come into his life who had offered him a path back to what he viewed as redemption. To rebalancing and justice. He might be unable by his own hand to destroy those who had wronged him, but this other had now taken on the task. He rejoiced now in another's efficiency, much as he had once in his own powers.

He imagined his protégée crossing through the garden, climbing the fire escape and entering through the window he knew was always slightly open, especially in the summer heat. He imagined the fans in the room, the soft whirring, casting currents of air adrift across the sleeper. And then it would be easy, the knife slipping beneath the ribs, into the heart. There would be artistry to it. And then the card would be left. It satisfied him that he could do no better job himself, that master had now become teacher and that one day his protégée would perhaps acquire skills even beyond his own.

CHAPTER 2

Alice Weston could never have foreseen the effect her work would have. She had taught adult education classes for fourteen years, exhibited in local and national exhibitions, and made up the rest of her income by running a tiny but well-thought-of framing shop and mat-cutting service. She had no family, and no one depended on her except the assorted art students who lodged in her spare room and helped to pay the mortgage. They came and went, and some even kept in touch for a year or two, but her social life was largely confined to the few close friends that she had kept since school and her classes — which she loved when they went well and hated whenever she realised that not everyone who passed through her doors possessed talent, some not even a modicum.

But now Alice's largely complacent little world had been shaken to its core, for Alice had produced something remarkable. Something which had pushed her right out into the public eye. She had created the Book of Angels as a gift for a friend and had coupled the traditional interpretations of the tarot with her own responses to her research for the project. Alice had always kept a journal and a dream diary, and as she had worked on the tarot, she'd become more and more aware of the way it had infiltrated her dreams. Of the way in which even the most casual journal entry had become infused with the meaning of it. On her friend's advice, she had tentatively offered the cards and her little book of interpretations and meditations to a producer of commercial packs, and she had been astonished at the response. They had wanted it, produced it, distributed it, and now Alice could go nowhere without seeing this strangest of her creations on public display.

And the feedback she was getting. Fan letters, of all things, forwarded through the agent she had somehow acquired. Regular emails which talked about the inspiration of her writing, the accuracy of the cards when used for divination, not to mention the insights it delivered and the way it helped people on their spiritual journeys. Alice was frankly baffled. What had started as a whimsical gift for a dear friend had changed her life.

And now she was being interviewed by the police.

DI Beckett sat opposite Alice Weston waiting for her to reply to his question.

'I know this must be hard for you, Miss Weston, and we are not implying your involvement. Not at all. But can you think of any reason, any at all, why this card should have been left at the scene?'

Alice Weston shook her head. 'It's not even a major card.'

'A major card?'

'Oh, it's the way the tarot is divided up. The Major Arcana have the deepest meanings and they're the most important when you do a reading. The card you showed me, she's called the Queen of Cups. It's . . . it's like the Queen of Hearts in an ordinary pack of cards. It represents an emotional woman, someone nurturing and caring, or sometimes a situation where emotions get the better of good sense. It depends which cards are next to it in the layout and what position it's in.'

Dave Beckett considered this for a moment. 'Do you actually read the cards, Miss Weston?'

Alice shook her head, her long blonde hair moving against her face, hiding much of her expression. 'I don't use them like that. In fact, I don't really use them at all. I made them for a friend. I just never thought . . .' She brushed her hair impatiently from her face and gazed in bewilderment at Dave Beckett. 'Do *you* know why, Inspector? I mean, why should anyone kill someone and then leave one of my cards on the body?'

'What makes you think that it was on the body, Miss Weston?'

The grey eyes widened. 'Oh, I just thought. I mean . . . Oh Lord, I'm digging a hole for myself, aren't I?'

'Are you?' Beckett let the question hang for a moment. 'We know you have an alibi for that night. We know that you were twenty miles away with a dozen witnesses, so why should you think that you're digging a hole?' He smiled at her, allowing his expression to relax for the first time since entering her house. 'We don't suspect you, Alice. May I call you Alice?'

She nodded, almost eagerly. 'Of course.'

'We don't suspect you,' he continued, 'but you are correct, though that knowledge is to go no further, you understand — that the card was left on the body of the dead woman. An elderly lady who could not have fought back.'

He watched Alice's expression. Her face had been pale to begin with, but now the colour drained completely. 'Can I ask how she was killed?'

He could see that the question was almost an involuntary one. She didn't really want to know. She didn't really want to have that image in her mind, but she couldn't help but ask. He had witnessed this contrary behaviour many times.

'A single stab wound. If it's any comfort, she was probably not even aware of the intruder in her room, and she died instantly.' He watched her swallow convulsively. He didn't think it *was* any comfort. 'If you do know, or think you know, why someone chose to leave this card, this card in particular out of, what, eighty?'

'Seventy-eight.'

'Right. Seventy-eight. So why choose this one?' Beckett waited again, realising that the questioning had once more come full circle and suspecting that this was all a waste of time.

Alice got up and began to pace around the tiny living room. She was a woman fast approaching forty, but she had changed little since her twenties, beyond the addition of a little weight and a few wrinkles. She still wore her hair long, though a few grey strands stood out among the blonde. It suited her, both in style and colour, and her deep-set grey eyes were gentle and expressive. Beckett found himself wondering why she had not married.

'It's used as a significator,' she said.

'I'm sorry? A what?'

She ceased her pacing and sat down opposite once more. 'Significator. Like an identity card. I don't read, but I learned how to while I was designing the cards.' She paused, frowning. 'The tarot is divided into four suits, like playing cards, except that they're staves, coins, cups and swords. And each suit has its court cards. King, queen, knight and page — the knight and page became the jack in the ordinary pack, historically. Well, not everybody reads the same way. Some people use the major cards as significators and some people don't think that one person has the same significant all the time, but commonly, when people read, they choose a card that represents the person they are reading for. The King of Swords would be right, say, for an older, dark-haired man, someone who is dynamic, businesslike, authoritarian. Pages are young people, children even. Knights more often young men than young women, though they can be either. You get what I'm saying?'

Beckett nodded. 'I understand. And the Queen of Cups?'

'Blonde, blue eyes or grey. My sort of age or older, though a lot of it is not about age but has more to do with life experience. And a woman who acts on impulse, lives life with the heart rather than the head and who is known to be warm and loving.'

Beckett nodded once again, his mind working overtime. The woman Alice Weston had described perfectly matched the victim in whose hand the Queen of Cups had been found.

CHAPTER 3

Ray had gone to Highbury House largely out of curiosity but also an odd sense of defensiveness on Lily's behalf. Lily Spencer, he decided, was a nice lady, the sort his mother and aunt would have been, had they still been around, and it wasn't good for nice elderly ladies to be troubled by charlatans with fancy playing cards.

Highbury House was Edwardian. An impressive building in one of the quiet streets off the London Road, it must once have been a family home, complete with servants. As Ray pulled into the in-and-out gravelled drive he caught a glimpse of what might have been a stable block beyond and extensive gardens.

It wasn't his usual idea of a retirement home, but then, if the residents were anything like Lily, it would have to be something a little different. He looked up at the cream-and-gold sign on the gatepost. It was not 'Highbury Care Home,' or 'Highbury Residential Something-or-other,' simply 'Highbury House,' as though any further clarification was no business of the casual enquirer.

The historic house boasted an impressive front door with a tiled step and stained glass. No ramp, Ray noticed, so either the Highbury folk were all steady on their pins or there must be another entrance, perhaps around the side.

The old black door opened freely, but inside Ray found himself facing a glass security door with a keypad and smart-card slide and a little notice that advised him to ring for attention. Having an eye to security issues these days, Ray was suitably impressed.

His ring brought a dark-haired lady in a pale blue dress out from a large room off to the right. Ray glimpsed a number of people sitting about in easy chairs before the inner door swung to and guessed it must be some kind of residents' lounge.

'Can I help you?' the woman asked him through the glass door. He felt her gaze rest for a little too long on his face. His burns had healed well, received in an attack while he had still been in police service, but the scars were still there, plain and ugly as the nose on his face. Ray had never been a handsome man, even before.

'I'm here to visit Lily Spencer,' Ray said.

The woman smiled. 'Oh yes. If I could just have your name?'

'Ray Flowers.'

She smiled again and pressed a buzzer which released the door. 'Come on in, Mr Flowers. Lily and her sister are all ready and waiting for you. You'll have to excuse the formality,' she added, gesturing towards the door, 'but some of our residents are a little worried about strangers these days.' She leaned forward confidentially. 'Especially with the murder, you know.'

For one awful moment, Ray thought that Lily's fears might have come true and Rose really had been killed off by the predicted maniac, but then, he reassured himself, the woman would hardly have mentioned her waiting for him had she been already deceased.

'Murder?' he asked.

'Why, yes, you must have seen it on the evening news. The local papers have been full of it. An old people's home in Mallingham. An intruder got in one night and stabbed an old lady in her sleep.' She looked askance at him, obviously regarding his lack of knowledge with some suspicion.

'I'm sorry, but I don't often watch the news these days and I'm at least three days behind with the papers.' Ray smiled, somewhat embarrassed. The truth was that since leaving the police force, he'd been rather inclined to ignore the news. Time was, he'd been featured in it far too much for his own comfort. He still endured a vague daily worry that Ray Flowers, either in the guise of hero — as had been the case after he had been attacked and burned — or as the whistle-blower and chief witness he had become, would become newsworthy again.

The woman awarded him another of her smiles, this one somewhat puzzled, but she'd evidently put her doubts about him on hold. She led him through to the residents' lounge, explaining as she did so that she was Sheila Ellington. She was in charge of 'this little family' and would be more than happy to talk to Ray later should he feel the need. They crossed the lounge to where Ray could see Lily sitting beside the sunny window.

'We're rather an unusual gathering,' she said. 'Most of our ladies and gentlemen were performers at some time. Show business, you know,' she added, in case Ray was in need of clarification. 'Most paid into a retirement fund while they were still working, so they could spend their declining years in a rather better location than the state pension might have allowed them to.'

Ray suspected this was almost part of the sales pitch, or some kind of habitual explanation for new visitors.

'They're quite a lively bunch most of the time.'

Ray nodded his understanding, reflecting that this was probably not a 'most of the time' afternoon. The majority of the residents appeared to be dozing in their chairs or chatting idly over afternoon tea. But, he admitted to himself, it was a pleasant enough place to doze, with its big bay window overlooking the front drive and open French windows leading down to the lawned gardens at the back.

Lily had risen to meet him, both hands outstretched in welcome. She looked as neat as ever in a simple green

13

shirtwaist dress with a little pearl necklace at the throat and matching earrings half hidden beneath her thick, white hair.

'Mr Flowers, I'm so pleased that you could come, and the timing is just right. Look, the tea is ready to pour and we have chocolate digestives and custard creams.' She gestured towards an empty chair opposite her own and Ray sat down. 'This is Rose,' Lily told him, but Ray could easily have guessed. The two women were as alike as peas, though Rose wore her hair up in a tidy chignon and wore yellow instead of green.

'You're twins.'

'Oh, quite,' Rose giggled. 'And very useful it was too, in our profession.'

'The two of you were on the stage?' Ray asked. 'Mrs Ellington said that a lot of her' — he wasn't sure what to call the inhabitants of Highbury House, 'residents' somehow sounding too institutional — 'her . . . guests had been in show business.'

'Oh, dear Lord, yes. Most of us. And we still do pantomime at Christmas, provided we can manage to stay awake.' Rose's blue eyes twinkled and she smiled at Ray. He found himself smiling back and wondering just what these two had got up to in their younger days. Come to that, what mischief they were capable of getting up to now.

A third woman was seated at the little table. She had busied herself pouring the tea, but she extended her hand now and Ray shook it. Her grip was firm and her steel grey hair cut in a severe style that did not entirely compliment her rather long face. She wore a tweed skirt, despite the heat, and a short-sleeved twin set with a Celtic-style brooch pinned at the breast.

'Elspeth Moore,' she announced. 'Pleased to meet you. You have a strong aura, you know. I'd guess you must be a pretty old soul. Do you ever dream about Ancient Egypt?'

Ray was not used to being called an old soul. Old other things, yes, but he didn't think that was quite in the same league. And no, he couldn't say he knew a lot about Egypt, ancient or otherwise, or that he had any shadowy memories of princedom there.

'Pity,' Elspeth told him, 'but no matter. You should try recording your dreams, you know. Very useful as windows into the unconscious mind. You'd be amazed at what stuff we all have hiding in our attics.' She tapped her close-cropped head. 'And never think you're too old to learn new tricks. Big mistake that, but a lot of us make it. I've discovered things about myself these past few months that you'd never guess.' She leaned forward, the two Spencer sisters copying her move. 'Thirty years in the business and' — she shrugged and explained in her low, rather hoarse voice — 'mostly, it's been cold reading, m'dear. You know, learning to work the crowd, pick up signs and signals from what they're wearing, what they say, how they look. But suddenly, there's no need of any of that.' She sat back abruptly, the sisters again mirroring her actions. 'If I were a few years younger, I'd take it on the road again. By God, the halls I'd fill now.' She put down her cup and spread her hands as though describing something large and very impressive. 'Elspeth Moore, Clairvoyant to the Stars.' She looked Ray in the eye and thumped the table hard enough to make the crockery rattle. 'By God, I would.' She leaned back into the easy chair with a reluctant sigh.

Ray sipped his tea, trying to think of something appropriate to say. He set his own cup down. 'What brought about this change, Miss Moore? Lily mentioned something about a new tarot pack, but I have to admit I'm as ignorant about the tarot as I am about the pharaohs.'

Elspeth grinned, showing a set of strong, if slightly yellowed, teeth, and Ray suddenly knew how it would feel to be confronted by a hungry shark. She reached down and brought onto her lap a voluminous leather and canvas bag, from which she took a small book and a silk-wrapped bundle.

Ray was afraid he knew what was coming next. And he was right.

'Best way is to show you,' she announced. 'Clear the top table, you lot,' she called out. 'Elspeth's about to do a reading.'

* * *

Ray did not like being the centre of attention at the best of times but he found himself with little option. Elspeth led him to the large, round table set close to one of the deep bay windows, and she sat him down and herself opposite. The Spencer sisters took the chairs next to Ray and, it felt, the entire company of Highbury House clustered around, some seated, some standing as Elspeth began.

Maybe they don't get many visitors, Ray thought. *Maybe they just haven't got out of the performance habit.* But whatever the cause, everyone seemed intent on hearing what Elspeth had to say. Ray wondered how much Rose and Lily had already told her and how much of his previous career would be rehashed in Elspeth's little display.

She surprised him, though. After unwrapping her cards from their silk packaging — 'protects them from the wrong psychic influences' — and shuffling them for a minute or two, Elspeth put them down and addressed Ray and the assembled company.

'Mr Ray Flowers has come here today to give assistance to our friend Rose. As you may remember, when I read for dear Rose on her last birthday, the reading was full of the most dire warnings, omens which I, as a conscientious medium, could not afford to ignore.'

A ripple of agreement rustled through the audience and Rose clenched her hands tightly together on the tabletop. Lily covered them gently with her own.

She's genuinely afraid, Ray thought. He frowned across at Elspeth, wondering if he should say something now, his initial prejudice against charlatans with fancy playing cards resurfacing with a vengeance. He bit his tongue. He wanted to see what Elspeth would do next.

'Our dear Lily went to the police, of course, but they were as much help as a cockerel in a pig yard, and until she was led to our dear friend Mr Flowers, all seemed pretty desperate.'

'Miss Moore . . . Elspeth.' Ray felt he had to intervene. 'I don't know that I believe any of this, you know. I just came because Lily asked me to. Because she was concerned about her sister.'

'You don't have to believe, Mr Flowers,' Elspeth told him. 'Only to observe. Then you must take whatever action you deem fit in the circumstances.'

'Please, Ray, just hear her out,' Lily whispered. 'It won't take much of your time.'

Reluctantly, Ray nodded. He didn't like the way that things were going and he promised himself a few strong words with Elspeth Moore before he left. Any amusement he had felt earlier had now evaporated. Big time.

'We know,' Elspeth continued, 'that Mr Flowers was himself a policeman. That he left the force and set up in private practice, as it were. And we are all still in agreement, I take it, that whatever fees are charged by Mr Flowers in pursuit of justice will be met by all of us?'

There was a general nodding and murmured agreement.

'Now, hold on—'

Elspeth held up her hand. 'Please, Mr Flowers, we are all in agreement. Just hear me out.'

'I don't mean to be rude, Miss Moore, but I told you I don't really hold with this, and I'm certainly finding it hard to accept that any sort of cards can foretell someone's death. I'm even more upset by the notion that you should then *tell* the person they are going to die. I mean to say, Miss Moore . . .'

'What would happen if that person had a heart condition, or was weak minded enough to curl up and die? Yes, yes, Mr Flowers, we've thought all about *that*, and if the reading hadn't been so damned persuasive, then I would *never* have told Rose that her life might be in danger. Never. But I ask you, Mr Flowers, what if I had ignored the reading and then something dreadful had happened to poor Rose? Would that have been ethical, even according to your exacting standards?' She shook her head vehemently. 'I don't think so.'

Ray didn't know what to say. He looked at Lily and Rose, who were watching him anxiously, then threw up his hands in surrender. 'All right. Do your reading, try to persuade me. Tell me why you think Rose might be in danger and I'll do what I can. But, Miss Moore, I'm warning you, I'm a hard man to convince.'

Elspeth nodded as if satisfied and then handed the cards to him. 'Shuffle. Then cut twice. And hand the cards back.'

Ray concentrated hard on shuffling. There were more cards in this deck than in a playing card pack, and his scarred hands, though fine for most daily tasks these days, still felt stiff and awkward when it came to dealing with more delicate work. He shuffled slowly, trying not to drop anything, and then laid the cards down on the pale blue silk and cut twice as he had been commanded.

'Good. Now, listen and watch.'

She laid the first card down at the centre of the blue silk and nodded her approval. 'Good. That's the fellow I would have chosen.' She gave Ray a shrewd sideways look. 'Didn't want to be seen to be leading the pack, you know. Too much like you leading the witness!'

Ray peered at the card, which seemed to show an armed man leaning on a rather impressive sword. 'I'm not sure I understand.'

'The significator, Mr Flowers. The card that represents the essential you. Usually, of course, *I* choose it first, the card I think is closest to the person I'm reading for.'

'And what if you don't know the person?'

'Then I use my intuition, of course. Now, King of Swords. A man of action. Also a man of law and good judgement. Someone who cuts through the Gordian knot of intrigue and sees straight to the solution.' She gazed about her at their assembled audience. 'Looks like we have the right man for the job, all right. Now, let's see what we have next . . . Ah! I might have guessed it would be.'

'What?' Ray wanted to know. Another figure with a sword, this time a winged figure with the blade raised above his head and a fierce look in his eyes that seemed to focus determinedly upon the viewer. An old-fashioned pair of balance scales were set upon the floor at the figure's feet, feet that were heavily booted and clad in spurs.

'The Angel of Justice, or the Avenging Angel if you prefer. The card of balance and order,' Elspeth told him. 'It's St Michael the Archangel, you know, ready to trample to death the enemies of justice and smite off their heads with his mighty sword. It's that concern with justice that led you to where you are now.'

Ray allowed a smile to tilt the corner of his mouth, wondering how she had palmed the cards after he had shuffled them. She was good, he had to give her that, and the images on the cards were impressive. He'd seen tarot cards before, but they were nothing like these.

'You're wondering how I palmed the cards.'

'Miss Moore, I . . .'

'No, man, of course you were. It's the way you think, the legalistic mind at work. I'd have been disappointed in you if it had been otherwise. Slip your damned scepticism back into your pocket for a minute or two and let me finish. The Angel of Justice tells me how you came to be what you are now. You've an instinct for the underdog, Mr Flowers, and a healthy disregard for the kind of petty proceduralism that your office might have employed. Now, let's see what came in your past.'

She laid a third card to the left of those in the centre. There was no figure involved this time but instead a tall and elaborately constructed tower standing on the banks of a rushing torrent. Impressive as the building was, its foundations were being undermined by the rushing water, even as the summit was destroyed by lightning, forking out of an otherwise clear and brilliantly blue sky.

'The Tower,' Elspeth said. 'The undermining of your world, your beliefs, the very substance of your life, and' — she pointed at the lightning — 'just when you think life can't get much worse, the lightning strikes from out of nowhere and really finishes you off. I'm presuming it was this incident that left you with your scars.'

Ray shifted in his seat. *Of course*, he thought. This was common knowledge. Anyone could guess as much if they'd read about him in the papers or even knew a little bit about his life over the past year or two.

She laid another card, this time to the right of centre. 'The Lovers. Someone who saved you from yourself and made you realise that none of it really mattered so long as you had her. Good for you, m'dear.'

Ray smiled in spite of himself, thinking that there were aspects of his Sarah's character that were not so far from those of Elspeth. The brusqueness, for a start. Maybe he should introduce them.

But Elspeth was frowning at the card and hesitating before she turned the next. 'I want to cover the card. I don't usually reckon on doing that, but there's another something or someone important in this position. It's . . .' She turned the next card and laid it sideways across the lovers. The figure in this card was ambiguous in its gender, riding a horse and carrying a large cup, overflowing with wine. 'Another woman.' It was clear from Elspeth's tone that she was puzzled by it. 'Quite a bit younger than you. An emotional woman, someone who feels too much and sometimes reasons too little, and I feel — not something the cards are telling me, you understand — I feel that's she's from the past in some way and that she's very spiritual.' She looked at Ray. 'You had a relationship with this woman, but you've spoken about it to very few people. Something extremely deep and painful, but you resolved it in your own mind, even if you did get the answer wrong.' She frowned again. 'I have the feeling that this woman has passed over but not yet gone, if you see what I mean.'

Ray was genuinely discomfited this time. She had to be talking about Kitty, though how this woman could possibly know so much about her, Ray did not begin to understand. He dismissed it immediately as just window dressing. She was right, very few people knew anything about Kitty and he was determined to keep it that way. There was no way this woman could have a handle on something like that. Ray had not believed in ghosts before he had encountered one in the cottage that his aunt had left him. It had not been a negative experience, not frightening, but definitely sad. It had also coloured Ray's judgement about subjects he had previously dismissed as rubbish. Fortunately, Elspeth Moore seemed ready to pass on.

She laid a card at the head of the cross she had begun to make. 'The Star. Hope springs eternal. See the bright Angel of Hope and Compassion hovering in the background? That's what's going on in your head just now, Mr Flowers. You're hopeful about the future. More hopeful, perhaps, than you've been since you were a little child.'

The last card completing the cross depicted yet another angelic figure, but it carried an emblem that Ray vaguely associated with Egypt. A pair of scales with a jar on one side and a feather in the pan on the other. The two objects finely balanced. The Angel was looking at the balance but it's — his? — free hand was outstretched, ready to grasp the hand of the figure emerging from an open grave close to its feet.

'Resurrection, Mr Flowers. A task or a cycle completed well so that another may begin.' She nodded approvingly. 'You've done all right for yourself, considering your problems, but there's still work to be done. A new task.'

'Isn't there always?' Ray asked. Elspeth glared at him and he immediately regretted his attempt at flippancy.

'Now,' she said. 'Let's see what else you're getting up to.'

The rest of the reading consisted of mainly what she called 'minor cards,' by which he gathered she meant those that related to the four suits in normal playing cards. She laid four at the side of the cross and talked at length about what he expected of life and what life should expect of him. 'Project the image of the Eight of Coins,' she told him. 'A craftsman who can well afford to be observed at work, who has nothing to hide and knows his job well.' Then she laid four more cards above the rest. 'To give a timescale to events. Watch carefully and listen, this is for your benefit and guidance.' She took a deep breath.

'In the next few days, the Page of Cups will rule. Not, in this case, a person, I don't think. Though, of course, it can sometimes represent a young person who is impulsive and reactionary but generally of good heart. In this case, I think it will mean time for contemplation. For weighing your thoughts. The next week will bring great change and a lot of hard work. See, the Chariot of Time rushes by and you'll barely have a moment to yourself, so make the most of the brief time before that happens. After that, in the next month, the Knight of Swords will ride back into your life. Noisily, if I know him — a young man, impulsive but with a quick mind, though he does not always make use of his experience and good sense. And the final card, the influence of the coming year, is the Wheel of Change. By the time the year ends, Mr Flowers, your entire world will have turned upside down. Again.'

* * *

There were always a lot of visitors on a Saturday and so it was often hard to find a private space in which to talk. He led them into the garden, down to the furthest corner, where folding chairs had been set out for residents and visitors. They were both here today, both girls, and he was very glad of that. His protégée was now demonstrating her skills, the other one was still at the beginning but it would be her turn soon. Today he was happy and sitting in the sun. In the dappled shade of an ageing tree, he felt positively vibrant.

'You did well, very well, very clean and neat. I've read all the reports, of course, but I couldn't wait to hear it from you. So tell me, did you have any difficulties? Walk me through it.'

She smiled, confident and very beautiful, he thought. 'I did my homework, I watched for several days first and I noticed that the landing window was usually left open at night. It's the one next to the fire door, so leaning over the fire escape railing, I could just reach to push the window further open and then it was a bit of a wriggle, but I managed to get in OK. There were fans on in the hall, just like you said there would be, and in her bedroom too. There's no air conditioning in the building and no one checks on the residents after eleven, unless they ring their alarms. So I knew it would be pretty easy, really.'

The old man regarded her sternly. 'Never assume that things will be easy,' he told her. 'I'm giving you simple targets now, but who knows what you might face in the future.'

She shrugged. 'I know, but it all went well this time. I went down the corridor. Hers is the third door and her window faces onto the front, but I couldn't get in through that window, obviously. That would have been good, but it's too close to the street. Anyway, she had a fan on in her room, but I opened the door slowly anyway, just in case it made a noise. She was in bed snoring, fast asleep, so it was really easy. I know, I know, it won't always be, but it was this time.'

The old man glanced across to his younger visitor. She had not spoken in quite a while, but there was nothing unusual in that. She never had much to say for herself. He just wished she wouldn't look so miserable. He had enough long faces around without her adding to it.

'How did it feel, when the knife went in?' He tried not to sound too eager, but this was what he really wanted to know. He remembered his own experiences, that moment when life was being extinguished but was not quite gone, when the power was his.

She thought about it. 'It didn't really feel like anything much,' she admitted at last. He was displeased by this apparent flippancy and could see she was aware of this. She said quickly, 'I was just focusing on getting it right, I didn't have much time to think about what I was feeling. I just wanted to get the job done and get out.'

He nodded, not entirely convinced she was taking this matter seriously enough. He turned to the younger girl. 'A masterclass in how it should be done, Fly. You can learn a great deal from your sister. Listen and learn, watch and learn. It will be your turn soon.'

'I don't want to.'

'Nonsense. That's what you're here for. I promised your mother I would look after you, and I will. You'll want for nothing; you'll have a better life than she had.'

He took a piece of paper from his pocket and studied it for a moment. 'Perhaps you'd like to do the honours, my dear.' He passed a paper and pen to his protégée. Two names had now been crossed off. One he had taken care of himself, Marilyn Simpson. And now he watched as she put a line through Cora Hudson's name. She passed the paper and pen back to him.

'And now, my dear, I think we should choose the next.'

CHAPTER 4

The past few days had indeed been busy. Elspeth Moore had been right about that. Several of the larger local companies still kept to the old industrial holiday of the July Fortnight, closing completely for the first two weeks of the month. This was a hangover from when Leicester had been a centre for hosiery and shoemaking and the Leicester Fortnight had been universal. Ray could remember from his younger days coming into the city in early July and finding it all but deserted, half the population having fled to Skegness or Mablethorpe for their annual dip in the freezing sea.

Late June and early July had been good for business last year, he remembered. Last year, as this, there had been new security systems commissioned to be installed in those two weeks when the factories were empty of workers. The groundwork had of course been done long since, but both Ray and his partner George took great care to check up on installation and to be available should problems arise, generally keeping an eye on work being carried out under the Flowers-Mahoney banner.

Their attention to detail had paid off too. Much of this year's work had come about from word-of-mouth recommendations from the year before and their combination of detailed, personally advised risk assessment and state-of-the-art technology was paying dividends.

They had moved from their original premises on the tree-lined Clarendon Park Road to these offices closer to town. Their first office had been in a prestigious area and had an address that had given just the right impression to prospective clients, but the offices had been much too small since they had acquired staff and the computer equipment, printers and cars that came with them — parking had proved to be a big problem, and they had really needed something more suited to their business.

It was Sarah who had found it. A lease had become available for a property on the London Road, not three-quarters of a mile from their old location. It was a noisier site, closer to the city, a few hundred yards from the station and on one of the main thoroughfares in and out of town. The offices were larger and had allocated parking spaces in a rear yard, which would solve the problem of street parking both for themselves and their clients — provided they didn't all own Mercedes or Jaguars. The entrance gate was, it had to be said, just a little narrow. But the thing that really clinched it was the history of the place. The first private detective agency in the city, comprising ex-police detectives 'Tanky' Smith and Tommy Hayes, had started life there. Busts of its detectives in their tall hats and various disguises proudly decorated the cornices of the impressive sash windows.

Ray had still found time to attend to the concerns of the Spencer sisters, though he remained unconvinced there was anything really to be concerned about. He'd left Highbury House with a vague feeling of unease, the cause of which he could not quite place. It certainly wasn't that he took Elspeth Moore's claims with more than a very large pinch of salt. But, as the everyday world had taken over once more, he had dismissed his troubled feelings and told himself that he had done his duty, and that put an end to the matter.

That hadn't stopped him, though, from phoning Rose and Lily every day to check on them, to ask about strangers coming to the house and, grudgingly, to approve their plans not to allow Rose out alone or to allow her to sleep without a personal alarm beneath her pillow. It also hadn't stopped Ray looking at media reports regarding the death of Cora Hudson, the eighty-two-year-old woman who had been stabbed in her own bed on the first floor of the home she had lived in for the past fourteen months. The news reported Cora to have been a lively and happy woman, enjoying the bingo and weekly dancing and exercise classes for residents. She'd ended up at the home because she'd had a bad fall and had been unable to return to her little flat. Staff described her as the life and soul of the party. It seemed that the killer had got into the home through a small window which happened to be next to a fire escape. The window was often left open at night, the upper corridor being stuffy and airless. A fan was kept running to draw in cool night air. That window, Ray thought, would now be kept firmly closed.

As June turned into an unusually hot July, and the little white council van that tested the air quality took up its usual position once more outside the funeral directors on the Welford Road, another death drew his attention and increased his anxiety.

The dead woman was seventy-two-year-old Bethany Himes. A widow who had gone into a home after her husband's death three years before. Years of nursing a man with Alzheimer's had taken their toll and, though not particularly old, her health had suffered and two minor strokes had convinced her that she no longer wanted to be alone.

Rosemeade was a private nursing home and Mrs Himes had sold up and invested the money from the family home, hoping that it would last her through her time. *It had certainly done that*, Ray thought sadly. There had been speculation as to who would benefit from her inheritance, speculation that was crushed when it was revealed that Mrs Himes had bequeathed her estate to various animal charities and had done so with the full blessing of one son and two daughters, all of whom perceived the selling off of the family home — and their inheritance — as a small price to pay for not having to care for an elderly mother who had shown every sign of 'going off like Dad,' as one of them candidly admitted.

By all accounts — and there were many, the second bizarre murder of an older lady in the supposed safety of a nursing home being of interest even to the nationals for a day or two — Mrs Himes had been generous and popular. She had enjoyed the company that her new life had to offer and was also, like Cora Hudson, 'a demon at the bingo,' according to one of her fellow residents who seemed deeply upset at such a promising new vocation being so cut short. Saddest of all, Ray thought, that she should have had only a few years of freedom after so many years of being chief carer and protector of someone everyone described as a difficult, confused and occasionally violent man.

'She was a lovely lady,' an old neighbour said. 'Would do anything for anyone.'

Even allowing for the usual platitudes, she didn't seem the sort to have attracted enemies or to have upset anyone enough to want her dead. There was the usual talk of drug-crazed youths and the moral decline of society. The usual declamations about old people no longer being safe in their own beds never mind out on the street, but the fact remained, buried in the tabloid hysteria, that Bethany Himes had not been robbed, despite there being both cash and jewellery clearly on display. Nor, despite hints to the contrary, had she been assaulted, beyond that one, precise stab wound which had probed beneath her ribs and stopped her heart.

It had taken Ray a day or so to decide to go further than simply researching what the media had to say, and he probably would have hesitated even longer had he not known the officer in charge of investigations. He was one of the few people left on the force who might actually deign to talk to Ray Flowers, ex-DI and general persona non grata. Ray had become acquainted with Dave Beckett the previous year, when they had met in connection with a series of ritualised murders linked to a religious cult called the Eyes of God. Ray had encountered the group eleven years before, when he had been on the team that had brought their leader to justice as a child murderer. The group had reformed and reinvented itself but doubts about them had still remained, and when a young boy had been found murdered, Beckett had been convinced he was investigating a copycat. It had become far more complicated than that and Ray still did not like to dwell for too long on the events that had followed.

Ray had been approached by Beckett because of his knowledge of the original case, and Beckett had continued to involve him in the investigation despite the opposition of his superiors, who were still reeling from the accusations brought against some of their number. The uncovering of such widespread corruption had demanded not just an internal enquiry but a public one.

Beckett was surprised to hear from him and was, as usual, pushed for time, but he listened to Ray's story without comment. 'You're number twenty-two, I think. Or it might have gone up since last week. That's when I stopped asking.'

'Number twenty-two what?' Ray asked, though he thought he could probably guess.

'Elderly ladies who have a premonition that they're going to be next. Oh, I'm not being flip, Ray, these people are genuinely frightened. I've assigned a couple of officers to fly the flag and offer a bit of reassurance, do a general security check while they're about it . . . when they're not dragged off on other jobs, that is. You know the score.'

'Yeah. I remember it well. Can't say I miss it either. Any more tarot readers among them?'

There was a momentary hesitation. 'Two, I think. Or one might have used a crystal ball. Most, it's just been bad dreams, odd men hanging about the neighbourhood. Wrong numbers and hang-ups on the phone. And you can bet your pension there's some little moron out there targeting folk he knows live alone and calling them for kicks. Look, it's out of our area, but I can arrange for someone local to talk to your lady, if you like.'

'What? And have you accused of stepping on local toes? No, don't bother, Highbury House is done up tighter than Fort Knox anyway. And I don't figure the residents of Highbury have too much faith in the local constabulary after they sent Lily on her way.' He hesitated. He'd got the feeling there was something Dave wasn't saying, that somewhere in their conversation he had struck a chord, but he was wary of asking straight out. In cases like this it was standard practice to hold back certain pieces of evidence, things that only the perpetrator would know, and Dave Beckett certainly wouldn't want to spring a leak in his own investigation, however well he and Ray got along.

'Are you connecting this with the murder of Cora Hudson?' Ray asked.

'Connections are being explored, let's say that.'

'Same MO? Or just same victim profile? From what I've read, it sounds as though the cause of death was very similar. Single stab wound. Whoever it is, they seem to know what they're doing.'

Beckett's reply was cautious. 'Let's say there are strong similarities,' he agreed.

'Was anything stolen?'

'Nothing. Both had money and valuables in their rooms, not a lot of anything but enough for a casual thief to have snatched. The motive seems to have been murder, pure and simple. Not that murder is ever pure and rarely simple.'

Ray thanked him and rang off, reflecting that Beckett must be pretty pissed off with the lack of action on the case so far. And it must be bad, as the police had so far put out three separate appeals for witnesses and were actively seeking to keep the case in the media for far longer than would be the norm if they had plenty of evidence already waiting to be sifted.

No, Beckett had run into a dead end on this one, Ray was sure of that, and the only consolation was that there had been no more action. More than three weeks had passed since the death of Cora Hudson and now the tabloids were having a field day with this second murder. Ray had noticed that there was even going to be some kind of television exposé about security in care homes. *Fat lot of good that will do*, he thought.

Maybe the tabloids were right. Some junkie broke in, intent on stealing, and got disturbed. Ray shook his head. How long did it take anyone to reach out and grab the cash and jewellery that, according to one report, had been lying on the dressing table?

No. It didn't go either with what Ray knew about burglaries or what he knew about addicts. Something like eighty per cent of all drug-related crime was committed by some five per cent of drug users. And they went for the easy targets. The odd mugging, a window left open, a car with saleable stuff left openly on the back seat. They didn't go to the bother of breaking into an old people's home to kill and then leave empty-handed.

Whoever had killed these two women had set out to murder, nothing more, nothing less, and Ray knew in his gut that it wouldn't be the last time.

He moved restlessly to the office window and tried to force them open even wider. Two fans were on full, but they made little impact on the temperature. It was late in the afternoon and the room had stored the heat of the day and was being slow to release it. His energy seemed to have been utterly sapped. And he was bored. Things had quietened down after weeks of frenetic activity, and there was nothing pressing left to do that day. George, his partner, was down in London, Sarah, an archivist, had left that morning for a conference on something archival and would be gone all week, and Ray felt out of sorts, too hot and frustrated that he couldn't figure out what it was that Beckett could be keeping back.

He slumped down in the captain's chair behind his desk and flicked through the day's papers that Rowena had left for him. Most of them rehashed what he already knew, but one small article on page eight of the *Mercury* caught his eye.

An old lady had died, he read, her body found by neighbours who had become concerned at not seeing her about. Police had broken in and found her two-days dead. The flies had beaten them to it and the heat had accelerated the putrefaction. Ray could just imagine the smell.

She lived on the first floor of a block of flats and she'd been so afraid of Bethany Himes's murderer that she had slept with all her windows closed. Ray knew the flats she had lived in. Built in a wave of seventies exuberance, they had picture windows floor to ceiling in the living room and main bedroom. *It would have been like an oven in there*, he thought. The theory was that she'd died of heat exhaustion, her body dried out by the sun streaming in through the expanse of glass.

Disgusted, Ray shoved the newspaper aside, mentally adding a third death to the murderer's score.

CHAPTER 5

It had taken a long time for Ray to get to sleep, the heat and the fact that Sarah was still away — he was no longer used to sleeping alone — making it hard for him to relax.

He slept with the windows wide open, the scent from the garden drifting up on the still, warm air, his sympathies going out to those like the lady who had died of heat exhaustion, too frightened to open their own windows. He and Sarah had bought this little cottage out at Peatling Magna a couple of years previously, and while the cottage itself was tiny, the garden was enormous enough for Ray to exercise his new-found passion for gardening. Ray would never have thought of himself as a gardener. Three years ago he barely knew a rose from a begonia, but then his aunt had left her house to him in her will. Mathilda had loved her plants and so had the previous residents of the four-hundred-year-old house. In trying to restore Mathilda's garden Ray had found himself hooked, and the yellow roses that now bloomed in this garden and were busy scrambling the walls outside of the bedroom window were kin to the ones Mathilda had planted in her own.

Ray still owned Mathilda's cottage. He had sold his own house and some of the capital from that had gone into Flowers-Mahoney, but he had never quite managed to get rid of Mathilda's home. Though he did not live there now, he made certain that the garden was kept in good order and paid the lady who had cleaned for Mathilda to continue to do her twice-weekly stint. He would rent it out, he promised himself, when the right tenant presented themselves. It would have to be someone special to be worthy of Mathilda's old home.

It was four in the morning when the ringing of the telephone woke Ray from what had become a deep sleep. For a moment he lay there, midway between waking and dreaming and unable to decide what the ringing was. Then he reached out and grabbed the phone.

'Ray? Oh Lord, I'm so sorry to have wakened you.'

'Lily? Lily, is that you?'

'Yes, yes. Oh I'm sorry, I should have said. Ray, it's about Rose. Oh dear, you have to come.'

Ray sat bolt upright in bed, fully awake now. 'Is she all right? Lily, what's happened?'

'Ray. Elspeth was right. Someone broke in and attacked Rose with a knife.'

CHAPTER 6

Ray arrived at Highbury House at quarter to five and pulled into the drive. Two police cars had been parked in front of the big front doors and every light in the building seemed to have been switched on. Light flooded out, illuminating half the street.

A uniformed officer stood just inside the door and stopped Ray before he could go inside, but Lily must have been watching for him because she burst out from one of the side rooms and dragged him in.

'I sent for him,' she told the officer at the door. 'He's our friend. *And* he's a detective, you know.'

Ray wished fervently that she hadn't said this, but Lily was quivering with rage and excitement and he didn't think that she was thinking all that clearly. He laid a calming hand on her arm. 'It's all right, Lily,' he said gently. 'Now where's Rose? You're sure she's not hurt?'

Lily nodded furiously. 'Oh Ray, it's been just terrible. This man broke into her room, and if it hadn't been for that alarm and for Elspeth with her cricket bat who knows *what* might have happened.'

'Elspeth? Cricket bat? Lily, what's been going on here?'

'Well, you don't think we'd let my sister sleep alone, do you? Not after what's . . . No, Ray, we've been taking turns and tonight Elspeth was sleeping in there. Sheila — Mrs Ellington, you know, she wasn't too sure, but like she said, they're our rooms and really, we can do what we like. She can't have the alarms on upstairs at night you know . . . Well, we're getting on a bit, some of us, and we forget to turn them off if we go wandering about. Not all of us sleep well, you know. Anyway, it's just as well we didn't leave Rose. Can you imagine?'

'Elspeth hit the intruder with a cricket bat?'

'Oh yes. That's what I've been telling you. She used to play in the ladies' county team, you know. And she'd have knocked him for six too, if it hadn't been for the curtains.'

'The curtains?'

'Well, yes. He tried to escape you see, after Rose set off her personal alarm. Lord, the noise of that thing! Have you heard one? Sounds like a banshee. Anyway, Elspeth grabbed her bat, but the lout was halfway out of the window and she couldn't get a decent swing. But she smashed down on his kneecap,' Lily told him proudly, imitating the gesture with both clenched fists. 'He'll be suffering! And quite right too.'

Ray was taking all of this in when a familiar voice sounded from the residents' lounge. Ray turned. Two men emerged through the double doors. One Ray did not know but he guessed he must be the officer in charge. The other was Dave Beckett.

'How long has *he* been here?' Ray asked Lily.

'Which one? Tall and skinny or short and round?'

Ray smiled. 'Tall and skinny.'

'Oh, he arrived not long before you did. The other one, he's called Fox or something. He's from the police station that told me not to be so silly and be on my way.' She straightened herself and squared her shoulders. 'And if they'd taken a bit more notice then, my sister might not have almost been killed!'

The two men glanced in their direction — Fox, or whatever his name might be, with the conciliatory smile already in place. Beckett, typically, did not bother, but he did have the grace to look surprised when he caught sight of Ray.

'Miss Spencer,' Fox began, 'I can understand that you're upset, but let me assure you . . . .' He paused and looked at Ray. 'And you are?'

'Mr Flowers is an ex-DI,' Beckett said. 'I believe that Miss Spencer asked for his help a few weeks ago. I'll vouch for him.'

Silently, Ray blessed Dave Beckett, but he could see Fox's eyes narrowing as he tried to recall where he had heard the name. He nodded at Ray. 'DI Fox. I appreciate your interest, Mr Flowers, but I can assure you, we've got it all in hand.'

'I'm only here because Lily telephoned me,' Ray told him. 'I won't be in the way. I expect there'll be a great many other concerned relatives and friends turning up during the course of the day.' He turned to Lily. 'I'm sure we could both do with a cuppa, Lily,' he said and took her by the arm. For a moment he didn't think she'd take the cue, but she hesitated only for an instant before patting his hand and joining with his play.

'Of course we could. We will be in my room, should anyone have anything useful to say.' And with a last rather contemptuous look at DI Fox, Lily led Ray up the stairs to her room on the second floor.

* * *

A quiet knock on the bedroom door some half an hour later announced Dave Beckett's arrival.

'May I come in?' he asked Lily.

'Of course, of course. Ray's been telling me about you. Says you have more sense than most.'

'Thank you.' Dave Beckett almost twitched a smile. 'Miss Spencer, your sister's finished giving her statement, I believe. She's still refusing to go to the hospital for a check-up but they've called the local GP and he says she seems well enough. She's asking to see you.'

'And you want a word with my detective,' Lily Spencer added for him. 'Well, thank you both, I'll let you use my room for your little tête-à-tête, but Ray, I'll be asking questions later. You may be sure of that.'

'I'm sure she will,' Dave Beckett mumbled when she'd gone.

Ray laughed. 'So you'd better tell me what I shouldn't repeat. I take it your being here means there's definite proof this is linked to *your* old lady and to the other one?'

'Unfortunately, yes. I was still hoping they would prove to be individual, isolated incidents, but there were too many similarities. I'd even have settled for the drug-crazed yob the press is so keen on. This is nasty, Ray.'

'What weren't you telling me the other day?'

'I wondered if you'd catch on.' He shrugged. 'Your tarot reader, Ray, what pack did she use?'

'What pack? Why? Oh, it was Angels something . . .' He thought for a moment. 'Book of Angels, that was it. Why?'

Becket's mouth tightened. 'I thought it might be. Look, Ray, what I'm about to tell you is being kept under wraps, though I doubt it'll stay that way much longer. Elspeth Moore found the card, so they'll at least know half of it.'

'Card? He left a card?'

'Must have dropped it this time. On the previous two occasions, he placed it in the dead woman's hand. Obviously, thanks to the lady with the cricket bat, he didn't get the opportunity.'

'Do we know how badly she hurt him?'

'We'll have to assume nothing was broken. He managed to get back down the drainpipe and make a break for it across the neighbours' gardens. We know which way he went, he tripped three security lights on the way.'

Beckett dropped down into the chair that Lily had occupied before he arrived and rubbed his eyes wearily.

'You have nothing, I take it.' It was not a question.

'Sweet FA. Three weeks in from the first death and there's nothing more concrete than we had on the first night.' He paused. 'I've had a chat to Elspeth Moore.'

'Bet that was fun. She offer to do you a reading?'

'No, she said my aura wasn't right. What do you make of her, Ray?'

'You mean, did she mastermind an attempted murder?'

'Or did she set something up just so she could be the hero? Seems a bit odd that she should be there rather than anyone else.'

'I don't know,' Ray said. 'How many were sharing the night watch?'

'A half-dozen, including the two carers on the night shift. They do sleepovers apparently, and they've been taking turns napping in Rose's room on a camp bed. So,' he asked again, 'reckon she's up for it?'

Ray thought for a moment then he shook his head. 'She doesn't strike me as an obvious suspect, but you never know with these things. And there is the link with the card, of course.'

Beckett laughed mirthlessly. 'You must lead a sheltered life these days. Have you any idea how many of those packs have been sold in the past six months? They're everywhere. I've even seen them for sale at my local filling station. The Book of Angels is the biggest thing to hit the shops since . . . since *Harry Potter*.'

'Harry who? Oh, that boy magician thing. I've not read the books but I saw one of the films when it was on the telly.'

'That's the ones, yes. I have nieces and nephews who wanted them for Christmas. Elspeth Moore read for you, did she?'

Ray shrugged. 'She didn't give me much of an option.'

'Obviously *your* aura was right.'

'Say what was wrong with yours, did she?'

'I'm not sure I want to know. How did she strike you?'

'You mean, did she tell me I was going to win the lottery? I don't know. Sincere, I suppose. She's sharp enough.

38

Admitted that most of what she'd done previously was cold reading — I guess what we'd call "copper's nose" — but she was adamant that what she did now was real. The cards guided her, she said. And I think she believes that.'

Beckett frowned. 'She didn't strike me as senile.'

'You don't have to be senile to believe you're psychic.'

'No, maybe not.' He smiled at Ray. A proper smile this time, crinkling the tired lines around his eyes. 'I'd forgotten you believed in all this occult stuff.'

Ray just laughed. 'I don't believe, necessarily, I've just learned to keep an open mind. What were the cards our killer left?'

'The first victim, Cora Hudson, she got the Queen of Coins. Bethany Himes got the Queen of Cups. This time, Rose seems to have been designated as the Queen of Swords. 'A capable woman with a sharp and incisive mind,' apparently.'

'Ah. Significator cards, yes?'

'Apparently. Elspeth Moore tell you that?'

Ray nodded.

'Well I went straight to the horse for my info. A woman called Alice Weston. She designed the damned things.'

'And?'

'And she was as helpful as I think she knew how to be.'

'You told her about the card?'

Beckett nodded.

'Could she have leaked it?'

'To a potential copycat? No, I don't think so.'

'Fingerprints?'

'No such luck. Not even a partial. Alice Weston gets a lot of fan mail, both physical letters and email. I've got someone working through those, but so far nothing useful.'

'But I suppose that might yield something eventually, the cards are obviously important to whoever is committing these murders, so I suppose there's an outside chance he might get in touch with their creator. If that's all you've got, though, you're really clutching at straws. And not much of a description either, Lily reckons. Elspeth said he was male, strong but not tall, and she thinks young, but he wore a ski mask.'

'That's more than we had for Bethany Himes or Cora Hudson.'

'Ah.' Ray sat for a minute or two in silence, thinking it all through. They really didn't have much. The cards. The bit of a description. The fact that the victims were elderly and lived in residential homes. Ray pushed himself to his feet. 'Coming?'

'Where?'

'To have a chat with Elspeth Moore. I want to know the layout of cards she had the night she read for Rose.'

'What! Ray, what possible help can that be?'

'You got anything better?'

Beckett shrugged. 'Forgotten you were a couple short of a picnic.' Leaving it at that, he followed Ray downstairs to find the psychic with the cricket bat.

CHAPTER 7

Elspeth Moore was in the residents' lounge, cricket bat in hand, demonstrating for the edification of her fellow residents just how she had thwarted the would-be murderer.

'They've certainly revised my opinions of the elderly,' Beckett whispered.

Ray laughed. Elspeth noticed them and crossed the room, striding confidently, bat in hand. She was still dressed for bed, in a full-length pink dressing gown and brown leather slippers.

'I did all right, didn't I?'

'You did, yes.'

'My old headmistress would have been proud.' She sighed and flopped down in the nearest chair. 'Don't mind admitting though, I've had enough excitement to last me.' She tapped her chest impatiently. 'Gets the old ticker going.'

'Are you feeling all right?' Ray asked her.

'Yes, yes, don't fuss. I've already had the doc give me a once-over. But beating off murderers isn't what you reckon to be doing at nearly eighty.'

'You never are,' Ray said, and meant it.

'I surely am! Two years to go and I'll have been eight decades on this earth, and I don't mind telling you, I feel it just now. I'll be heading back for my bed very soon and staying there probably until lunchtime. Now, what can I do for you two gentlemen?'

'You found the card,' Beckett said.

'I did. Queen of Swords. The card I use if I'm reading for Rose. For Lily too, if it comes to that — there's not much to choose between them when it comes to intellect.' She looked speculatively at Dave Beckett. 'He left one before, didn't he? I've been thinking it through and that's what I've decided. He left a card before and that's what made them call you. Otherwise, they'd have passed it off as just another burglary, despite the fact that he was waving a knife around.'

Beckett nodded. 'I'll have to ask you not to share your thoughts.'

'You don't have to ask. I've got more sense than that. They're remarkable things you know, these cards, and your murderer obviously thinks so too.'

'Perhaps,' Beckett conceded. 'What we don't know is why.'

'He reads them,' Elspeth snorted, as though it was an obvious conclusion. 'Reads them and decides who it is he's going to kill.'

Beckett moved restlessly. 'I don't think . . .' he began, but Elspeth was waving his objections aside.

'Don't have the energy left to sit here and argue with you,' she said. 'But remember, I told you. You might have to think again.'

'Do you have your cards with you?' Beckett asked her.

'Why? I've already told you I won't read for you tonight.'

'I don't want you to. I want to know if they're all there.'

'You what!' Elspeth stared at him in blank surprise. She laughed. 'So, I'm a suspect, am I? Right you are, up the stairs with you. Let's go and check.'

Elspeth's room was on the first floor close beside the lift. Her room was similar in layout to Lily's, almost square but with the little bathroom set off to the left, not the right as it was in Lily's room. It was furnished almost identically but with the addition of an ancient chest of drawers that must be

Elspeth's own and a couple of rather elegant wooden chairs set beside a card table in front of the window. The walls were festooned — there was no other word for it — with photographs and framed invitations and yellowed newspaper clippings recording Elspeth's cricketing prowess and her psychic demonstrations. The bookshelves beside the bed were overladen with fat paperbacks and the odd larger hardbound volume, the content of which seemed pretty evenly split between cricket and the occult in one form or another.

Elspeth crossed to the table by the window and sat herself down. The deck of cards in its blue silk wrap lay on top, ready for her. She unwrapped them and spread them face up on the tabletop.

'Queen of Cups,' she announced. 'And there she is, the Queen of Swords. Check them out, Detective. See if I've switched them. Though I have to say, Inspector Beckett, if you think I can afford to buy two packs just so I can leave a couple of cards at a murder scene, then you've no concept of what the government pays us for the privilege of being old these days.'

Beckett examined the cards carefully and then handed them to Ray, who looked without comment. The wear from handling seemed about equal on all of them. There was certainly nothing discernibly different in the two Elspeth had named.

'And now, gentlemen, if you don't mind, I'd like to get some sleep.'

'I've just got one more question, Elspeth.'

She eyed Ray. 'And that is?'

'The layout of the cards the night you read for Rose. Can you remember it?'

Elspeth snorted again. 'Good Lord, man, I've been to bed since then! Oh, all right, all right, just let me think a minute.'

She spent several moments staring at the cards and then began to shuffle them about on the tabletop, sorting through for the ones she wanted.

'Queen of Swords as significator, of course. Then the Chariot, I think, and in the past the Magician and then the

Five of Swords . . .' She carried on, talking softly to herself as though that helped to clear her mind. 'There,' she said finally. 'Near as I can remember, that must have been it.' She watched critically as Ray noted the positions down and the names of the cards laid out. Beckett raised an eyebrow, clearly amused.

Afterward, as they were standing in the entrance hall at Highbury House, Beckett asked, 'You surely don't think there's anything in this?'

'The reading? Probably not. But you have to admit, she had a point. The killer must attach some importance to the cards, probably *does* read them. Learning about them might give an insight into his state of mind.'

'When d'you take your psychic exams?' Beckett shrugged. 'Oh, I know you're probably right,' he added, 'but you know how I feel about that sort of thing. Load of bollocks designed to separate the stupid from their money.'

'You'd regard Elspeth Moore as stupid?'

'Only in that one regard. Aside from that, I think she's remarkable.'

'And as a possible suspect?'

'As a possible suspect she is *still* remarkable.' He glanced at his watch and wriggled his shoulders to relieve the tension in them. 'Seven forty. Briefing at eight fifteen with Fox's lot.'

'You don't like him?'

'I don't dislike him. At least he's being cooperative. And you, what will you do now?'

'Have a word with Rose and Lily before I go, then get to the office. I've a full day.' Ray shrugged. 'Lily came to me for help, but I didn't take any of it seriously and someone tried to kill her. I don't like coincidence and, despite what you might think, I'm not ready to count Elspeth's predictions into the equation. There must be a link, a connection between Rose and Cora Hudson, Bethany Himes and our killer.'

'He'll try again,' Beckett predicted. 'Oh, I don't mean Rose, though I think we should keep a weather eye out. And next time there won't be an Elspeth Moore with a cricket bat waiting for him.'

CHAPTER 8

The old man had been waiting for news but the news when it came was not what he wanted to hear. He had been puzzled when nothing had come on the local radio in the early bulletins, then infuriated when it became obvious that the only thing of interest was a reported break-in at Highbury House residential home.

'What went wrong?' he demanded when Fly eventually called him. 'I couldn't have made it any easier for you.'

Fly, standing in the living room of her half-sister's flat did not know what to say. Her knee was throbbing where it had been whacked with the cricket bat and she was shaking so much she almost dropped the telephone.

His protégée took the phone from her, motioning her aside. She spoke quietly to the old man, calming his anger and telling him that things sometimes went wrong, he had said that himself. That it was Fly's first time, and usually people built up to something like this, going through the motions first before committing. Eventually she hung up.

'It'll be all right, he'll calm down, you'll see. Best get ready for school or you'll be really late. What have you got first period?'

'Maths. I hate maths.'

'I hated maths too. I learned more after I'd left. Grab your bag and I'll give you a lift, otherwise you'll be late. You've got money for lunch?'

The absurdity of the questions hit Fly forcefully. Who cared if she'd got money for lunch when she'd tried to kill someone the night before? 'I can't do this.'

Lynn hugged her. It was a perfunctory hug but a hug nevertheless, and these days Fly was grateful for what she could get. 'Forget it just now, I'll talk to him. Now come on, school. You're calling in to see your mum on the way home?'

Fly nodded that she was. The one good thing in her day. Which wasn't saying a lot, really.

A few minutes later she was dropped outside the school gates. The final bell was ringing and a few stragglers were making their way inside. Fly joined them, a small figure, too small for her age, wearing school uniform that hung on her too-thin frame. Fly wore everything looser than she needed it to be, it was her way of hiding. But she was beginning to realise that it actually drew attention.

She entered the classroom quietly, the lesson just about to begin. First-period maths was in her own form room, so the form tutor, who also happened to be the maths teacher, was giving out the morning notices. 'A reminder that next Friday is non-uniform day, and then the end-of-term activities in the afternoon. You will not be leaving early, the school day will end at three thirty, as usual. Final projects need to be in by Wednesday next — don't be late, late submissions will have their marks capped. Now . . .'

Fly glanced around to see what books everyone else was getting out and then copied them, pulling a maths textbook out of her bag, finding an exercise book. She sat alone at the back of the class. Trish, who was about the only girl in the group that was kind to her, smiled from the second-to-back row, glanced at Fly's books and pointed to her own exercise book. Fly had picked up the wrong one. She delved into her bag again, grateful that somebody had noticed. And then she tuned everything out once more, staring at the textbook and trying to make sense of the equations.

What did equations matter when she'd tried to kill someone last night? What did any of it matter anymore?

* * *

Beckett did not hang around for very long after the briefing with DI Fox and his team. He made a brief statement about the death of Cora Hudson, ensured that they had up-to-date details of the case and arranged for anything that came up with regard to the attack on Rose to be sent through to him. He returned to his own office some twenty miles away in Mallingham, a small and somewhat rundown but ancient settlement just off the A46, between Leicester and Nottingham.

After updating his own team, he made himself some coffee and retrieved Alice Weston's fan mail from the files. Most of it was printouts of emails. She had given permission for the police to access her professional inbox, the one relating to the Book of Angels website. And there was also a public forum which related to insights and readings and beginners' guides, that sort of thing. He had been surprised that someone as successful as Alice Weston seemed to be still living in the little terraced house that she had bought years before, but Alice simply liked the area. She'd lived there for a long time, she had local friends. But he also gained the impression that she did not trust success, that she felt that something that had come out of nowhere could equally well disappear without warning.

He had looked through her fan mail before but found nothing of interest. The emails were mostly complimentary. There were the occasional but inevitable abusive ones from people who were against anything that smacked of occultism or what they viewed as anti-religious activity. Alice admitted that she didn't read any of the emails particularly closely. She put broad responses on her website every now and again,

thanking people for their input and answering general que-
ries that people had made, but that was all. She would engage
only as far as she absolutely had to. Also on her website were
links to interviews she had done, and to various publicity
drives her agent had instigated and to other sites of readers
who made a habit of using the Book of Angels. She had told
Dave Beckett that her agent had found someone to build and
run the website for her and this seemed to be her only real
expense in terms of what she was prepared to do to market
her product. Beckett got the impression that Alice would
have been quite happy for none of this to ever have happened
— that she had been quite content meandering through life,
painting and framing and teaching and not being rich but
living very much on her own terms.

Well, that didn't work out, did it? Dave Beckett thought. Her
artistic endeavours had taken on a life of their own and she no
longer controlled them or what other people did with them.

He turned to the letters and the cards she had been sent
via the agency. He'd wondered if they'd weeded out anything
particularly offensive or difficult, but he had called them and
been told that no, they just redirected the mail. Alice said she
had a clear-out every few months, archived her emails and had
a bit of a bonfire. She'd sounded a little embarrassed about
this and mumbled something about not being able to keep
everything, but Beckett had gained the impression that any
novelty there might once have been in receiving these missives
had now worn off. Now she went through the motions before
dumping everything in a box, pending destruction.

Beckett could not help but wonder if some potential
clue might have gone up in flames.

Glancing through the cards and letters he noted a pre-
ponderance of roses and lilies. Flowers in general. Some of
the cards were rather beautiful and had clearly been chosen with a spiritual message in mind. There were standing
stones and stained-glass windows and a few of Glastonbury
Tor. Inside were general expressions of thanks and wonder
for the most part, some mentioning specific events that had

apparently been foreseen or problems that had been avoided. The letters were slightly more forthcoming, often relating whole incidents over several pages. Beckett was struck by their overall sincerity and by the fact that these rather strange cards seemed to have had an impact quite at odds with their modest and rather retiring creator. No wonder she felt out of her depth.

He set aside a couple of letters that seemed to warrant a little more attention. The police constable who had previously gone through had done the same and had followed up as far as she could, where a return address had been supplied. It was difficult to be subtle when introducing herself as a police officer and saying, 'I understand you wrote a letter to Alice Weston about her fortune-telling cards.' One woman had been absolutely distraught that the police thought she was stalking poor Alice. Another was furious that Alice might have reported him to the police when all he'd done was send a nice letter of thanks.

It had taken a fair amount of diplomacy to smooth things over.

The two letters that Beckett had singled out had been received recently — Alice had forwarded them in the last few days. Both looked to have been written by the same hand. The thing that stood out for Beckett was that after the rather profuse expression of thanks in both, the writer had instructed Alice to watch the news.

It was a pity, Dave Beckett thought, that there was no return address on either envelope, and no clue whatsoever as to who the sender might have been. The postmark on one was smudged beyond recognition — it's looked as though someone had dropped it in mud and then trodden on it — and the second indicated that the letter had been posted somewhere in Birmingham, which wasn't really much help. But he set them aside all the same. It gave him the vague sense that he had achieved something that morning, albeit nothing that actually pushed the case any further on.

* * *

Evening found Ray working late clearing up last-minute paperwork. He had called Highbury House three times during the day and been assured that Rose, Lily and Elspeth were all recovering well from their ordeal. The police presence had continued for most of the day and all the residents had given statements, though for most all they knew was that they had been woken by a screaming air horn loud enough to give the frailer of their number heart attacks.

He had wandered into town that afternoon and had bought a pack of cards, the Book of Angels and the guidebook that accompanied it. Feeling somewhat odd about such a purchase, he had left it in his briefcase until everyone else had gone, then made himself a pot of tea and settled down at his desk to analyse what Elspeth had told him about the reading she had done for Rose.

Ray began to shuffle through the pack of cards, getting used to the feel of them between his hands. He felt clumsy and awkward, his fingers like sausages, scarred sausages at that. He laid the pack down and fanned it out across the table, searching for the cards that Elspeth had indicated she had drawn for Rose.

At the centre was the Queen of Swords. The significator, Ray remembered, and its meaning: *a strong intellectual woman who cuts through to the root cause of any problem*. Well, that sounded like either Rose or Lily.

Then the Chariot, a Major Arcana card. Ray skimmed the meditative interpretation and skipped down to the mundane. *Hard work and a long journey, but one which is enjoyable and which pays dividends in the long term.*

Simple enough. No doubt both twins had worked hard. He hoped they felt their rewards had been good.

The card that crowned the reading was the Five of Swords. Ray looked at its position to check what it meant before dealing with the meaning. '*The head card*,' he read. '*Revealing your immediate thoughts*.' And the mundane meaning of that, '*Niggling doubts and worries. Conflicts with friends which you would do better to avoid*.'

So, Ray thought, *according to this reading, Rose had arguments and conflicts on her mind.* Had she been worried about something? Well, nothing so far seemed to add up to a prediction of murder.

The card that fell below the significator was, Ray felt, a little more sinister. An image of death, winged and equipped with a sharpened scythe — the Death card or, as it was called here, the Angel of Transformations. And transformations rather than dire consequences seemed to be what the mundane meaning at any rate delivered.

Ray sighed, already frustrated and a little bored. He wasn't cut out for the mysterious. To the left of the significator fell the Magician. *Quite appropriate*, he thought, *considering their profession.* And to the right, the Ten of Swords, which Ray had assumed represented conflict and quarrels even before he consulted the book.

The little guidebook was clearly presented, with the picture of the relevant card on one side and a meditation on the other outlining the more spiritual and complex meaning of each card, followed by a simpler, everyday interpretation.

The page for the Queen of Cups, for example, gave as its simple meaning: *an emotional woman, giving, caring but whose heart rules her head.* The more complex spoke of deep emotional commitment and finding the heart of change. The interpretations for the major cards were more detailed and more complex. Ray skimmed them briefly before setting the book aside and scrutinising the cards once more. He wondered which interpretation the murderer adhered to. Ray made a bet with himself that it would not be the mundane.

He poured himself some more tea and sat back in the captain's chair admiring the rich design of the cards. The woman who had done the artwork was clearly very skilled. They reminded him of the title characters in illuminated manuscripts, possessing that same richness and complexity of design, the colours glowing with an inner life all their own. He picked up the book again and studied the larger versions of the pictures. Some of the detail was lost in the reduction — the fineness of the brushwork on the clothes and the magnificence of the flowers and the zoomorphic forms that almost faded into the background. Ray wondered how long each one had taken the artist to complete. It had clearly been a labour of love. Such detail spoke of something far more time intensive than commercial concerns would have allowed.

Ray was drawn from his reverie by the sound of a motor-bike on the road outside. It was an unusual sound and one with which Ray was all too familiar, the *thump* of the big British single. Ray got up and went to the window knowing what he would see. The red-and-chrome machine glowed in the afternoon sun, the rider in black leathers despite the heat. Ray watched him unfasten his helmet, lift it from his head and turn with the same movement to look up at the window.

'Nathan,' Ray breathed.

CHAPTER 9

Nathan had changed little since Ray had last seen him more than eighteen months before. Slim and pale, he gave the impression of being taller than he was simply because he carried himself that way. His hair had grown. Dark and wavy, it reached past his shoulders, but the remote blue eyes whose gaze seemed never to rest anywhere for long were just the same.

Somehow, Ray thought, Nathan was one of those people who never looked right *inside* of anywhere. He was too restless, too fey.

'What are you doing here?' Ray wanted to know. 'Beckett is still looking for you.' Nathan had fallen foul of a Beckett-led investigation and the DI was, Ray knew, still not totally convinced of his innocence.

'He has too many other things to think about,' Nathan said. 'Anyway, I never really went away. You just stopped seeing me, that's all.'

Ray sighed. Not able to think of a suitable answer, he went through to the tiny kitchen to put the kettle on. When he returned Nathan was standing by the desk studying the cards.

'Can you read those things?'

'I read the tarot,' Nathan told him. 'These are not the same.'

'They're similar though.'

'Similar, yes.'

Ray had forgotten how hard it was to get a straight answer. 'See anything there that points to a murder?'

Nathan glanced at him but did not immediately reply. He fanned the remaining cards across the table and selected one, exchanging it with the card at the base of the cross and then, after a moment's hesitation, switching that one with the card second from the bottom of the right-hand column. Ray came over to see what he had done.

The Death card now lay in the right-hand column, the Tower having replaced it at the base of the cross.

'So, what does that mean now?'

Nathan glanced up. 'The Tower is at the base, the foundation of all that is done. Everything that has been achieved was built on false foundations. And there is death in the environment. Death as settlement.'

'Settlement? Settlement of what?' Ray sighed. As always, when he talked to Nathan he felt reality drifting away and losing itself somewhere over the horizon.

'What could Rose Spencer possibly have to settle?' he asked again.

'A debt,' Nathan told him, as though that were obvious. 'Everyone must settle their debts, Ray. Even those they do not know they owe.'

'Now you're losing me. I don't get this stuff, Nathan. Give me a witness statement and a set of fingerprints and I'm happy. This lot isn't for me.'

Nathan nodded. 'I need food, and a place to sleep. But I will stay and help. I think you need me.'

CHAPTER 10

Ray had been surprised to get Beckett's call and even more surprised to have received an invitation to meet in the Jack in the Green that night. The pub in Mallingham was close to where Ray had grown up, though many of the households it had once served were long gone, their homes demolished in the drive for redevelopment that was currently wounding Mallingham badly enough to kill it dead.

He had wondered briefly what to do with Nathan and settled for ordering him a takeaway from Ray's favourite Indian restaurant on the Welford Road and leaving him to his own devices. Nathan, after all, spent most of his life alone, and Ray didn't think that another evening of the same would make any odds. He'd left Nathan eating prawn biryani and studying the Book of Angels, a combination which Ray was sure could not be good for his digestion.

Beckett was late. Ray sat alone in the corner of the lounge bar and watched the door, listening idly to the murmur of conversation. In Ray's youth there'd been a yard outside with benches and wooden tables for the kids to sit around and a swing made of an old tyre tied up in the elm tree. He'd often played there on summer evenings, sometimes with his dad, sometimes with the other kids while their parents were inside. The elm tree had succumbed to disease, and though the yard was still there it was now used as a car park. Two years ago the body of a child had been found lying beneath one of the old tables stacked against the wall. Ray took it personally that such a savage act should have taken place on his old home turf. He'd not been near the place since but felt that Dave Beckett's choice of this location for their meeting was an acknowledgement of their shared experience.

Beckett arrived twenty minutes late. He nodded towards Ray and gestured towards his drink, asking if he wanted another. Ray shook his head. He didn't drink much anyway and had the drive back to consider. He pulled out a chair. Beckett sat down with a sigh that was enough to deflate him.

'Long day?'

'Still going on.' He lifted his glass and saluted Ray. 'Don't suppose you privateers know about that.'

'We privateers know when we're on to a good thing. I was up as early as you though.'

'That you were.'

'So. Not that I don't like your company, but what did you want to say to me?'

Beckett smiled. 'Never did have any social graces, did you?'

'Never saw the need.'

'What do you know about the Spencer sisters?'

Ray shrugged. 'Probably as much as you do. Lily came to me to say she thought something was going to happen to her sister. The only evidence she had was Elspeth Moore's reading, but there's no mistake, she was very worried. I've told you all this. I went to visit, did some poking around, came up blank and very nearly dismissed it. Then someone tried to kill Rose.'

'We don't know that. Officially, it's still down as burglary.'

Ray snorted into his beer. 'You believe that, you'll believe anything. You think the press'll believe that then you're in the wrong job.'

Beckett smiled. 'No obvious enemies. No obvious reason for anyone to do either Cora Hudson or Bethany Himes any harm. Two elderly, inoffensive ladies with nothing to say why anyone would want them dead.'

'I asked Rose if she knew anyone in Mallingham and she said no. As far as she could remember she'd never even been here. Did the first victim, Mrs Himes, have family or connections with Leicester?'

'Nothing that we can turn up. Her family live in the Nottingham area. She and her husband lived in Mallingham all their married lives. He grew up here, she came from Plumtree just up the road. He worked in Nottingham and she did part-time jobs after the kids grew up. She was a full-time housewife and mother before that and then, of course, he fell ill, and for the past eight years she'd been a full-time carer. What about the first victim, Cora Hudson?'

'Lived alone till she had a bad fall a couple of years ago. She broke her hip and had a long spell in hospital. When she came out she wasn't confident enough to go back home and ended up in residential care. She seems to have been perfectly happy there though, organising everyone in sight. She was well liked. No close family, never married and no children. The manager of the home showed me Mrs Hudson's old photo album. She seems to have worked on cruise ships a lot, a steward or something. There were pictures from all over the world.'

Ray nodded. 'The Spencer sisters were southerners. Born in Plymouth, if I remember right, and travelled quite a bit until Rose decided it was time to settle down. Lily didn't, so I understand, but you can't imagine anything much different from that pair and Bethany Himes.'

'You like your old ladies,' Beckett said, clearly amused.

'Watch it. You'll be getting me a reputation. I like the Spencers. They're an eccentric pair, real characters. So is Elspeth Moore, for that matter. Anything more on the murderer?'

'Nothing helpful. We know he was young. Not tall but wiry, and he must have been reasonably strong. It's not an easy climb to Rose's window.'

'Must have landed all right, though. He was able to run away.'

Beckett nodded. 'There's a tentative sighting on the day Bethany Himes was killed — two youths hanging around. The residents said they seemed to have been drinking and were being rowdy. Nothing really to connect them with anything, but we're going through the motions.'

'It's a big step from drunk and disorderly to premeditated murder.'

'Premeditated?'

'Oh, come off it. How many opportunistic housebreakers do you know who read the cards first and carry a spare pack around with them just in case? No, our boy knew who he was going to kill. She fitted the profile.'

'From what I understand, so would a quarter of the female population. There are four significator cards. Four queens. At rough estimate, one in four women would fit the bill.'

'You reckon? You met many women lately? The Queen of Cups is a warm, generous, giving woman, remember.'

Beckett laughed. 'I still reckon it's like horoscopes. One in twelve is bound to be a Cancerian and of that lot someone's going to match the prediction. Law of averages. And anyway, think about the Queen of Swords. What woman is going to deny that they're intelligent and quick witted or whatever it means?'

'OK. Point taken. But our killer doesn't think like that. Our killer chooses, precisely. Question is, do they choose the victim first or the card? Which way around do they make the match?'

'If that's your only question . . .' Beckett was silent for a moment. 'You're supposing there's no connection between the victims and so probably no real connection between the victims and the killer.'

Ray nodded. And if there was no connection between either victims or killer, where did that leave the investigation?

It was everyone's nightmare, a random killer. Someone with their own agenda but whose rules were impossible to define. 'One thing that militates against that though,' Ray began.

'And that is?'

'That whoever our killer is, he must know enough about these women to choose the right card.'

'Not necessarily. Remember what I said about generalities.'

'True, but women *are* different, Dave. Some women run their lives according to the heart, some think and plan their way through. Some batter on a problem until it gives in, like the Queen of Wands, some deal with the materialistic side of life better than most. Whoever our killer is has to see those traits clearly enough to make a decision.'

'Possibly. So you reckon we're looking at, say, a care worker. Or a frequent visitor.'

'But, you're going to tell me, you've already run a check on anyone who's worked in both places and drawn a blank.'

'So far, yes. But we've still a way to go. For what it's worth, I think you're right. I *hope* you're right. I hope we have a connection, however bizarre. I don't want to think about the alternative.'

* * *

Ray called to see the Spencer sisters on the way home. It was late, but he guessed they'd still be awake and so they were, sitting with a small group of others in the residents' lounge . . . and playing poker.

'Is that allowed?' Ray wanted to know.

'So long as we don't do it for money,' Lily told him. She sounded quite regretful.

'You don't play pool as well, do you?'

'Do I look like a hustler?'

'Well . . .'

Lily laughed at him. 'I'm better at snooker, though only if I'm wearing heels. Five foot two isn't a good height for reaching across the table.'

Ray sat himself down beside Rose. She sniffed at him suspiciously. 'You've been drinking, Mr Detective.'

'Guilty, m'lud. I've just had a word or two with DI Beckett.'

'Oh? And did he know any more than he did this morning?'

'Not a great deal I'm afraid, Rose. It's not likely your attacker will come back again, you know. You must be shaken by all this but I'm sure you're safe enough now.'

Rose patted his hand. 'You're wondering if we're all up at eleven o' clock playing poker because we're afraid to go to sleep.'

He smiled. 'I wouldn't blame you.'

'Well, we're not. We often sit up late. We often sleep late in the morning too. We got into the habit years ago when Lily and I worked the evening show and then, if we were lucky, had some young gentleman take us out to dinner.'

Lily giggled. 'That usually gave them a shock. They'd see us up there on the stage and not know we were really *two*. You should have seen their faces when we both turned up.'

'We're on film, you know,' Lily said. 'You should see it some time.'

'I'd like that.'

'You'll have to wait until we can find a new projector,' Rose added. 'It's all the old reel-to-reel stuff, you know.'

'Have you thought of transferring it to digital? I know someone who specialises. They do a good job on restoration too.'

'Really? Does it cost a great deal?'

'I don't know, but it would cost nothing to take a look.'

Lily placed her cards face up upon the table. 'Royal flush,' she announced.

'You must be joking,' another of the players said. 'That's your second this evening.'

'Luck of the draw, I suppose.' She smiled at Ray and pushed herself to her feet. 'I'll go and get the recordings, and there are a few other odds and ends I think you'd like to see.'

When Ray left ten minutes later Rose and Lily and company were still playing cards, and Ray was loaded down by a box of souvenirs, mementos of Lily and Rose Spencer, performers extraordinaire.

* * *

Nathan was still in the office when Ray returned to check on him. He had fallen asleep on the uncomfortable sofa in their waiting room. Ray made them both tea, settled in the opposite chair and reported on his meeting with Beckett.

'This person will kill again,' Nathan said.

'Undoubtedly. You think these victims are picked at random or is there some plan involved?'

Nathan considered. 'I think the person who planned this knows who he wants to kill.'

'The person who planned this?'

Nathan shrugged. 'The food was very good. Should I sleep here?'

'No, you'd be uncomfortable. Look, you've heard me talk about my aunt Mathilda's cottage? I think it's best you stay there. I can let the cleaning lady know you're going to be there. Her name's Evie Padget but she won't be in tomorrow. I'll give her a ring and tell her a friend of mine will be staying for a while. I can drop by and bring you groceries in the morning, and you'll find clean sheets and such in the cupboard on the landing.'

Ray took the spare key from his keyring and Nathan considered it, as though keys were a mysterious thing.

A few minutes later Ray watched as he rode away. *What's brought him back?* Ray wondered. *Probably just some sixth sense that he was needed — that would be just like Nathan.* He found he felt rather glad about it, whatever the mechanism was. No one was better than Nathan at understanding the otherworldly and the strange.

CHAPTER 11

That morning, just before the daily briefing, Beckett received news of a five-year-old cold case. He had put out a call for any murders where a card of any kind had been left, deliberately not specifying what kind of card he meant. He wanted to cast his net as wide as possible.

So far it had brought up several cases where business cards had been found at the scene and turned out to be incidental. There were a couple where playing cards were present, one because the victim had been playing solitaire and another that was totally unexplained. But this cold case was different. The card left had been identified as belonging to a tarot pack, and five years ago the Book of Angels was still new enough not to have been immediately recognised for what it was. Besides, the court cards looked broadly like most other tarot court cards.

The victim was an eighty-three-year-old woman called Marilyn. She had been resident in a nursing home and was very frail and ill. Cause of death was a single stab wound, and her death had occurred in the half-hour gap between welfare checks. No forensic evidence had been found, nothing except the single card. The case was still open.

It was, Beckett thought, clearly related to the deaths of Cora Hudson and Bethany Himes.

But why the gap? This one killing five years ago, and then two deaths and one attempted murder now. It seemed like a very odd pattern.

He managed to catch the detective who had been SIO before he went into a meeting, and a quick conversation confirmed that the details between all three cases were very similar indeed. Case notes would be exchanged, cooperation was agreed, and Dave Beckett hung up thoughtfully. It had been announced that morning that a major incident team would be put together. It looked like they now had an additional case to add into the mix.

* * *

The old man had led Fly into the conservatory. Late evening, and the sunroom was deserted. He rarely took Fly back to his own room. He rarely took anyone there. In this place where private space was at a premium, he preferred to keep *his* private space that way, even if the visitor was the nearest thing to family he had.

He was still annoyed with her but conceded that maybe he had pushed her too far, too fast.

'Too impulsive,' he declared. 'Much too impulsive. How many times have I told you, it's all in the planning?'

'I couldn't have known,' Fly protested. 'That old bag with the cricket bat — she were waitin' for me.'

Fly winced at the memory of it. The knee was still swollen and blue with bruising.

The old man sighed. 'Just sit down.'

He regarded Fly. 'Do you remember the first time we met? You were just a tiny little girl, your mother brought you along to see me. You ate ice cream and sat on my knee. You were such a solemn little thing, but I could see something special in you, even back then.'

Fly nodded; she did remember. She had been five and her mother had been diagnosed with cancer for the first time, but of course she didn't know that then. She knew only that her mother was ill. It had been a terrible time for Fly, her mother in hospital and no one to look after her, and she'd been placed in a foster home for a while. Scared and confused, she really hadn't settled, and it was after her mother had come out of hospital, far too soon everyone said, that they had gone to see this old man. Her mother had promised that she would never be left alone again, never entrusted to strangers.

'It was when Mam was ill,' she said. She didn't really see the relevance and she didn't really like to think about that time. It was bad enough that her mum was ill again, and this time she wouldn't get better.

'I have to think,' he said.

They seated themselves either side of a little table and the old man took the ornate pack of cards from his jacket pocket and laid them down between them. He no longer needed the book. The words had been committed to memory long since. He shuffled slowly, his old hands twisted with arthritis, the blue veins standing proud through skin that was thinned by age.

'Now watch.' He laid the cards one by one upon the table.

Fly watched, looking at the pretty patterned cards and waiting for the old man to disclose their meaning.

'A long journey,' the old man said. 'To find a Queen of Staves. A long journey north, I think. And . . .' he laid the final card. 'The Sun, the Morning Angel. Success, Fly. This time, there will be success.' He reached back into his pocket and took out a list of names. Cora Hudson and Bethany Himes had been struck through in red, together with another that Fly could not make out. Rose's name had been circled. He ran a shaking finger down the list and finally stopped at one name, tapped it thoughtfully. 'This one next, I think. This one will do. Erica Trimble. Yes, she should be the next.'

'And the other one?' Fly wanted to know. 'What about the bitch what got away?' Her anger was directed more at the woman with the cricket bat than the one she had failed to kill.

The old man winced and looked reprovingly at the girl. 'Language! Manners maketh man, Fly, always remember that. We'll go back to the other one later, don't you worry. And next time, you'll get your preparation right.'

CHAPTER 12

Erica Trimble was dreaming about past glories. Her grand-children had been to visit and she had spent two happy hours that afternoon telling them about the time she ran away to join the circus and spent two years riding an elephant to open the show and high-kicking her way around the ring in the grand finale. It had been a supremely happy time in Erica's life, though she couldn't recall another time when she had worked so hard, not even when all three children were tiny and their father worked all the hours God sent just to make ends meet, leaving Erica to raise the kids and take in outwork, thronging and lacing shoes for the local factory to help the family budget.

They didn't believe her, of course, her grandchildren. They loved the stories, always begging for more, but their otherwise vivid imagination could not quite stretch to see-ing granny on an elephant. Not the granny who had worn white gloves for church every Sunday grandpa had been alive and helped out at endless charity jumble sales and who wore frocks almost down to her ankles even on hot summer days.

Erica doubted her children believed her either, though they did know it to be true. They had even seen the few faded photographs that Erica had saved.

Mostly they, like their father, chose to ignore their mother's wilder days. After all, they had happened long before her children had been born, before she met their father, with his kindly but rather puritanical ways. Before Erica had become Erica Trimble and been plain old Erica Jones.

Erica's room had a small balcony which looked out over the gardens. The residential home was only five years old, and most of the rooms had been built so that there was somewhere for the residents to sit outside of their own space. Erica had had to sell her home when she moved in here, a thought which still rankled. She would have liked to have been left with something to give to her beloved grandchildren. Most of all, she missed her garden, with its bright flowers and shady tree and little wooden swing. The home had gardens of its own, which Erica enjoyed and, she had to admit, she would have been heartbroken to have seen her garden go to rack and ruin now she could no longer care for it herself. The arthritis in her knees and hips made even walking painful, and her hands were too tight and too tense to pull the weeds and tie in the roses and all of the little jobs that she had so enjoyed.

And so, her tiny veranda was the limit of her floral world.

This night, she went out as she always did to water her plants and smell the evening air perfumed by the night-scented stocks and the evening primrose and admire the brilliant colour of the brash red geraniums that tumbled from the rail. And Erica remembered. Remembered Daisy the elephant and Pat and Josie and little Mary and all the girls who she had known and danced with and gone out with to chase the boys, and she wished that she had her time over again, just so she could have more of those sweet memories instead of two short years that had had to last a lifetime through.

CHAPTER 13

Ray was incredibly happy that Sarah was home again. She'd enjoyed her conference with a series of seminars on research and history but she too was happy to be home. They ate breakfast on the patio outside the kitchen door and Ray brought the box of memorabilia that Lily and Rose had lent to him for Sarah to look through. He planned on taking it into work that morning and giving it to Phil, their IT expert, to see what he could do with it. Phil had done a good job transferring old media into digital formats for a number of their clients, and so Ray was quite excited about what he might manage to achieve for the Spencer sisters.

Sarah flicked through the photographs, faded sepia and black-and-white, of two glamorous women in rather scanty costumes. 'Magicians' assistants. You know, I always fancied that when I was a kid, all dressed up in sequins and feathers, it looked so glamorous. Then someone explained to me that you spend most of your time crammed into a tiny box trying to avoid swords and pointy sticks and I went off it a bit.'

'Apparently, the fact that they were twins was useful when it came to disappearing acts,' Ray said. 'You'd like them, they're real characters. And as for Elspeth Moore, you know who she reminds me of — that actress who played Madame Arcati in *Blithe Spirit*.'

'You mean Margaret Rutherford. Goodness, she must be fun then.'

'A woman of very decided principles, I would say. Anyway, I must be going. I gave Nathan a ring and he's fine for supplies. The village shop is providing everything he needs and he's apparently getting on fine with Evie. He really needs to eat more, though, he's as skinny as that feral cat you used to feed.'

'I can meet you for lunch if you like. I'm covering at the city library this week, remember. They're short-staffed over the holidays.'

'Not sure I can manage lunch; I don't know how long my meetings will go on. But I can meet you after work and we can eat in town.'

He bent to kiss his partner, reminding himself that he was a very lucky man.

The past two days had been quiet. Beckett had called a couple of times and told him about the murder five years previously, but beyond that it seemed there was nothing new. He had men still carrying out house-to-house enquiries, others tracking anyone whose name appeared in Bethany Himes's address book or might have been mentioned in letters. They interviewed tradesmen who called at the homes, residents, visitors, staff, and then they interviewed them again, and Beckett had officers visiting Highbury House on a regular basis armed with names and photographs just in case someone's memory should be jogged.

Officially, publicly, the Highbury incident had been listed as an attempted break-in that had gone wrong, and the finding of the card was still kept under wraps. Apart from that, there were no further developments, and no connection, however tenuous, had been established between Marilyn Simpson, Cora Hudson, Rose Spencer and Bethany Himes. The list of victims was getting longer, but there were few clear leads in sight.

Ray gathered that Dave Beckett was more and more coming around to the idea that this was a random thing. That the killer had none of the usual motives. Had no reason that he would be able to fathom. He didn't put this into words, but Ray could feel it, that unspoken, unspeakable suspicion that hung between Beckett's words whenever he rang.

Nathan spent long hours studying the cards and guidebook, an occupation Ray had been ready to abandon after that first night. What he gleaned from all this, Ray wasn't too sure. He said little, but when Ray had visited the cottage Nathan had shown him a pamphlet from a seminar given somewhere about the Book of Angels, so Ray assumed he must be taking his studies fairly seriously.

Ray had been amused by how well Nathan and Evie seemed to be getting along — the one so taciturn, the other who'd win gold if talking ever became an Olympic sport.

'Where *have* you been living?' Ray had asked him, knowing that his old home had been destroyed during the investigation into the Eyes of God, but Nathan had simply shrugged. 'All places,' he'd said. 'Anywhere I could park my bike.'

His bike was currently parked in the back garden of the cottage, a piece of cardboard stretched beneath in case of oil leaks. Vintage British bikes, Nathan told him, could be relied upon to leak. Nathan had also busied himself in the garden, weeding and planting, deadheading the roses. Somehow Ray had never imagined Nathan gardening. He was too much a creature of shadow and silence to look right in a sunny garden filled with the sound of birds.

Driving off to work on that bright sunny morning, Ray speculated uneasily that nothing much would happen to help break the case until another attack occurred. One that might bring a witness forward. It was not a pleasant thought.

CHAPTER 14

Lynn had driven and Fly had bunked off school for the day. She wasn't sorry about missing school but she wished it had been for another reason.

'What if I mess up again?'

'We talked about this. You won't. She's just one dumb old lady, she won't put up a fight. You just walk up, you do it and you walk away. Just prove you can, Fly.' Lynn cast an anxious glance in her direction. 'Look, try not to think about it too much now. See how you feel when we get there.'

Fly shrugged. 'You know he's nuts, don't you?'

'Maybe. He doesn't have the same moral compass as most people, if that's what you mean.'

Fly laughed. 'No, he's just fucking nuts.'

'Don't swear, you know he doesn't like it.'

'He ain't here. Anyway who cares if he doesn't want us to swear, he wants us to kill people. What's it matter if I swear?'

Lynn had no answer to that. After a little while she said, 'How's your mum doing?'

'Not good. The doctors say it won't be long now. She's just skin and bones, she can't hardly breathe.'

'I'm sorry, kiddo. I know how much you love her.'

Fly swallowed hard and tried not to cry. 'What happened to your mum?'

Lynn shrugged. 'Buggered off with some other man when I was fourteen. I stayed with my dad, then got a place of my own.'

She makes it sound so easy, Fly thought. She supposed it was just so easy for the Lynns of this world. People who didn't care about anybody or anything. Though she had been kind to Fly in that almost absent way that people are kind to cute dogs or kittens or even small children.

'We'll be there in a few minutes,' Lynn told her. 'Now, just take your time, you've done all the preparation, you can only do your best.'

It sounded so much like the advice Fly's mother gave her whenever she was about to take an exam that Fly wanted to laugh and cry all at the same time. Or maybe just grab Lynn by the back of the neck and ram her face into the steering wheel over and over again. Desperately, Fly hung onto that feeling, that momentary rage. Maybe if she could find that again, keep it, she could do what she had to do.

* * *

Erica Trimble looked up. A small, slight figure had just appeared in front of her and was blocking out the warm rays of the afternoon sun.

Erica squinted at the haloed shape. Her eyes, tired from an hour of gazing into the bright blue sky through the red filters of her closed lids, could make out only a silhouette almost black against the light.

'Are you looking for someone?' Visitors often wandered out into the garden looking for their relatives. It would not be the first time that afternoon that Erica had had to redirect them.

The figure shook its head. 'Lookin' for you.'

'For me?' Erica lifted up a hand to shade her eyes and the figure swam slightly further into focus. 'Do I know you?' she enquired.

'No. You don't know me.'

'Then . . . I'm afraid I don't understand.'

'He said it would be easy,' the figure said. 'But it ain't. It ain't, is it?'

Erica stood up, disturbed by the strangeness of this small person no taller than Erica herself. She moved around so that the sun no longer shone in her eyes, though her vision was still blurred and the colours all wrong.

'Who are you? What are you doing here? This is private property, you know. I could call the police.'

Fly stared at trainer-clad feet, shuffling nervously. Fly's knee hurt still from the encounter with the cricket bat and the knife in Fly's hand felt heavy and unwieldy.

'Are you all right?' Erica Trimble asked. 'Maybe you've been out in the sun too long.'

The small figure shook its head then shoved a hand into the pocket of its jeans and pulled something out. Erica Trimble started back, alarmed as her unwelcome guest lunged forward, the thing it had taken from its pocket clutched in its hand.

Erica screamed out loud as something was thrown towards her, hitting her sharply upon her temple.

Then Fly turned and ran . . . and Erica Trimble carried on screaming until help arrived and someone led her back to her chair and sat down beside her, patting her gently upon the hand.

'It's all right, dear, it's going to be all right,' the care worker told her gently. When she had walked by ten minutes before, Erica had seemed in a deep sleep. She must have had a nightmare.

'Didn't you see him?' Erica whispered. 'Didn't you see that . . . that . . .'

'It was only a bad dream,' the care worker soothed. 'You must have got up not fully awake and thought . . .'

'There!' Erica shrieked triumphantly. 'Look there. That proves there was someone. They threw that and it hit me just beside my eye.'

The carer looked to where Erica was pointing and picked up the thing lying on the ground. It was a playing card, she thought at first, plain on the back, just blue with a black border running around the edge. Curious, she turned it over. The Queen of Staves, dressed in a purple robe and carrying a crowned wand, stared out imperiously from a pale gold ground.

CHAPTER 15

When Maggie had called and asked if Ray might be free to drive her and the kids to the amusement park, he hadn't been too keen. John had been called away, she'd explained. She didn't want to disappoint the kids and, to be truthful, Ray was her last hope.

It was affection for Maggie and her family that had led Ray to agree, so he figured that same affection must be responsible for the position he was in now. He had this awful feeling that Sarah would be laughing her socks off when she found out, and he made himself a promise that love or friendship, wonderful as those things were, would never again persuade him to do anything else as silly as this.

Behind him, Maggie's kids, Beth and Gavin, were giggling and cheering as the rollercoaster was winched higher and higher, backwards up a near vertical slope. 'One hundred and twenty-five feet,' the man on the loudspeaker announced cheerfully. 'Sixty miles per hour straight down when the winch is released.'

Ray stared hard at the treeline on the horizon, his hands clenching the harness that strapped him rigidly into his seat. Ray tried hard not to think about how much he hated heights.

Then the damn thing was released. Ray Flowers plunged down the one hundred and twenty-five feet at sixty miles per hour and was then flung unceremoniously upside down through a double loop, wrapped around a corkscrew and shot back up yet another hundred-and-twenty-five-foot slope.

Ray caught his breath. All around him people were screaming in that mix of terror and delight that characterised theme parks. Behind him, Beth and Gavin still giggled. Ray was fairly sure that he hadn't screamed, so far, though as the ride suddenly released again and shot him backwards through the corkscrew and the double loops, a certain amount of sound was inevitably squeezed from his reluctant lungs. He hoped fervently that it sounded like a masculine roar of approval, not the rather pathetic squeak of protest that he suspected.

He was shaking head to toe when the children helped him off the ride, pausing briefly to tell him how great it had all been before shooting off to buy keyrings complete with photos to commemorate their ride.

'Did the big, brave policeman have a bad time?' Maggie asked him sweetly, taking his arm and leading him down the steps to where Nathan waited, silent and impassive as usual.

'I noticed you sidestepped that quite nicely,' Ray said. 'I thought you were coming on too.'

'Do I look stupid?' She grinned at him. 'John loves the infernal things, so do the kids. He was really sorry to have missed today. Me, I like my sky the right way up.'

Ray laughed, feeling a little better now that his feet were back on solid ground. Nathan was watching him.

'Why don't you try it?' Ray asked the younger man.

Nathan shrugged. 'All right.'

He went to join the queue. The children, seeing another opportunity to ride, ran to join him, first pressing their new keyrings into their mother's hand.

'Well, I'll be . . .' Ray said, watching Nathan being strapped into the car, Beth at his side and Gavin behind. 'I'd never have thought he'd . . . What's so funny?'

Beside him, Maggie was giggling wildly. She held out one of the keyrings the children had just bought. It showed both children with broad smiles on their faces, their arms stretched up into the air, clearly having a wonderful time. And Ray, head ducked down between his shoulders as though he were trying to hide and his eyes tight closed. His mouth was open though, and Ray was suddenly disillusioned about his memory of the masculine yell.

'Just don't show it to anyone. Ruin what little credibility I have left.'

Maggie laughed again and tucked the offending pictures into her bag. 'I'm sure Sarah would love one of these.'

Ray considered his skills as a pickpocket.

They watched as the cars were winched up again, the children laughing, Nathan totally impassive.

'Doesn't he ever smile?'

Ray thought about it. 'I'm not sure he learned how. Doesn't mean he's miserable though. He's just Nathan. I suppose being brought up to believe you might have to be the new Messiah is a little sobering.'

Maggie gave him a puzzled look. 'Should I ask for an explanation of that?'

'Probably not. He was one of Harrison Lee's kids.'

'Ah, well that's enough to scar anyone.' Maggie fell silent for a moment watching the cars go through the corkscrew and back up the second slope. Nathan, so far as they could see was still impassive.

Ray and Maggie had known each other for almost three years. They had met when Ray had gone to live in Mathilda's cottage after being released from hospital. In those days he had been so very conscious of his scars, of what they did to his face, turning his mouth into a lopsided clown's when he tried to smile, stiffening his features and making his hands clumsy and awkward. These days he went for long periods of time barely thinking about them, noticing again only when people stared. And even then, he paid them little mind. He had learned that he was more than the sum of his physical injuries. Much more.

Maggie and John had become friends, a first for Ray, who'd never known a vicar before. But then, he reckoned there were not too many like John Rivers.

'What's on your mind?' Maggie asked him. 'Apart from keeping your breakfast in the right place?'

Ray smiled. 'A couple of elderly ladies, actually. Or rather, a trio, if you include Elspeth Moore. Maggie, do you know anything about the Book of Angels?'

'That tarot card thing? Not much. I read an article in a woman's magazine, something about people who'd had lottery wins after reading the cards, but I wasn't paying much attention. Then John had an odd experience. One of his parishioners bought a pack and apparently got such convincing results she scared herself silly. She insisted he take them from her. I think they got shoved in the kitchen drawer.'

'*Your* kitchen drawer? Then it might be ten years before you find them again.'

'I'll have you know I tidied. *Recently*. You might excavate them in, oh, as little as five.'

Nathan and the children had returned. To Ray's surprise Nathan was clutching a photo keyring in his hand. Ray looked at it. Nathan, as stern and composed as ever, stared out with restless eyes. It occurred to Ray that this was probably the only photograph in existence of the young man Harrison Lee had created to be the next Avatar.

'You actually liked that?' Ray asked in disbelief.

'Beth says that I must try the others,' Nathan replied. 'I think I might.'

He was led away, a child on either side of him, grabbing his hands and pulling him towards the next ride. Ray shook his head.

'It'll be good for him,' Maggie said. She took Ray's arm again. 'Something tells me he hasn't had time yet to be a child.'

CHAPTER 16

Beckett called him and told him about Erica Trimble. This attack was out of his jurisdiction and had emerged because he had put out his general request for information about attacks on the elderly, particularly those where cards had been left at the crime scene. At least this time it had not taken five years for a connection to be made.

'But she's all right?' Ray wanted to know.

'Shaken, but the doctor's seen her and she's fine, physically. Her statement is going to be faxed through, but from what I've been told she woke from a doze to find someone bending over her. She couldn't see clearly because the sun was behind them, but she felt scared and stood up. He threw the card at her and ran away, but Mrs Trimble swears he had a knife in his hand.'

'And that's it? No description?'

'Small, light build, fair hair, she thinks, though as I said, the sun was behind him. But he spoke to her.'

'Spoke to her! And said what?'

'That he'd come to see *her* and that something wasn't easy. You have to understand, Ray, she's very shaky. All they've got is a provisional statement and I haven't even seen that yet. I might not have heard at all, but some young PC saw the card and remembered a memo that had been sent round. The home is sixty miles from here. We're lucky they made the connection and it wasn't just passed off as another loony on the loose.'

'OK. So when do you go up to see this Mrs Trimble?'

'Hopefully tomorrow, provided she's fit enough to talk to me. I'll keep you informed. One thing worrying me though. A lot of people saw that card, and there's been a good deal of media coverage on the Bethany Himes murder. It only takes one leak and the whole thing will be out.'

'Is that necessarily a bad thing?'

'Depends how it's been presented. If the media say there's been a cover-up, that we've not revealed everything that's in the public interest, *then* we've got a problem. Personally, I think we should pre-empt. The only reason we kept it quiet was in case we made an arrest, you know that. It was something only the killer would have been aware of. That's not going to be true anymore and we're no nearer to making an arrest. I'm tentatively inclined to go public now.'

'I agree, though you'll have every crank, everyone who has a grudge against their local fortune-teller, every religious nut phoning in and reporting on their neighbour. There must have been millions of the bloody things sold.'

'So I believe, and I know the downside, but I think we're left wide open anyway. I'm going to see Alice, the designer — suggest she goes away for a few days, just in case this information does break.'

'Good thinking. I don't suppose she ever expected to get tied up in a murder investigation. Why didn't he kill Mrs Trimble?' Ray wondered.

'How should I know? Attack of conscience? Or maybe he only kills people in their sleep. Maybe if she hadn't woken up, she'd be dead by now.'

* * *

Fly had been taken to see the old man. Lynn was waiting for her in the car. They had driven back in stony silence and then come straight here.

'You didn't do it, did you?'

'I went, didn't I? I left the card.' Fly clenched her fists, trying to sound more confident that she felt. She wanted to be anywhere but here. She was so scared her chest felt tight. Her stomach was turning over and she wanted to be sick.

'And you left her alive. That's twice you've failed, Fly, and I couldn't have made it easier for you. Two frail old ladies and you couldn't even get that right.'

'The one that hit me weren't that frail.' Again she took refuge in anger. He seemed to understand anger far more than he understood weakness.

'The old woman that hit you wasn't the target. Fly, when you came to me, when your mother sent you to me, it was so that you could learn a trade. Earn a decent living and make a proper life for yourself. We're family, Fly. You and Lynn, you're my heirs. My blood.'

Fly shrugged. 'Mebbe.'

'What do you mean, maybe? What did your mother tell you when she sent you here?'

'That you knew my dad. She didn't say nothing about you being family.'

'Well, you should believe it, Fly. I'm kin to you and I made a promise to your mother years ago that I would be responsible for you, and soon, when your mother's gone, I'll be all you have left.'

CHAPTER 17

The day after he had heard about Erica Trimble was a busy one for Ray. A blue-chip company at the new science park wanted George and Ray to give a presentation alongside a local risk assessment specialist from the Scarman Centre. If they took up with Flowers-Mahoney it would be the biggest contract so far. Both had had their mobile phones switched off and so they had returned to the office before Ray found out that Elspeth Moore had called four times.

He phoned her straight away.

'What's wrong, Elspeth? Is someone ill?'

'No, no, nothing like that. I've had another warning, Ray. The one that attacked Rose, he'll be back.'

Ray sighed inwardly but promised to go round that evening. It had been a long and somewhat tedious day and one in which many of the issues had, frankly, gone right over his head. They'd taken Phil with them as the major concern for the company was one of IT security — this was Phil's domain. It was Phil who had undertaken the task of converting the reels of film Rose and Lily had entrusted to Ray.

Ray had tried hard to listen to the talk of firewalls and optimum connections, but felt he had contributed little and that Phil and George alone could have handled things better.

The emphasis at Flowers-Mahoney had shifted in the past eighteen months, he thought, largely since Phil had come on board full time. To begin with they had dealt mainly with the physical side of security, vetting would-be nightwatchmen, recommending and designing alarm systems, that sort of thing. Lately the emphasis had been on the more esoteric side, and Ray was not certain that he liked the change, however profitable it might be.

He'd given a lot of thought to carving out his own niche within Flowers-Mahoney, but as yet, he wasn't certain what.

In some ways, Elspeth's call was a welcome diversion and after dropping Phil back at work, Ray went over to see her.

Elspeth had left the cards set up on the table in the bay window.

'See,' she said.

Ray looked, trying to recall what each of the cards meant. He saw the Death card, the Angel of Transformation. And the Devil or Constraining Angel, binding a human figure tightly in chains. Two small figures in the background seemed to be arguing. One was wielding a knife. A card he guessed must be the Knight of Cups — he had no idea what that one meant — and others, like the Five of Swords which he had seen in the earlier reading.

'I'm sorry, Elspeth, I have been trying, but you'll have to tell me.'

Elspeth sighed and sat down on one side of the table, directing Ray to the other.

'The central card,' she told him, 'is the Death card, the Angel of Transformation. Transformation at the deepest level.'

'But that doesn't always mean physical death,' Ray pointed out. 'I did get that far.'

'No, no it doesn't, though in our present context I think I might be forgiven for taking it more literally. Crossed by the Knight of Cups. That's the person who attacked Rose.' She looked puzzled, as though the card didn't strike her as quite right.

'The card at the foundation is what would be the Devil in the ordinary pack, what here is called the Angel of Constraint. Someone is being compelled to do this, Ray. Someone who doesn't know how to escape from the task set.'

Ray looked sideways at her. 'You're telling me our killer's being forced somehow?'

'Or they feel they are. Compulsion and constraint can be two sides of the same coin, you know.' She pointed. 'Then it's crowned by the Tower. So far, the purpose has been undermined.'

'By a lady with a cricket bat.' Ray smiled.

'One does one's best. The past is full of confusion, see the Seven of Cups. Too many choices but, because of the constraining factors of the Devil, there's been little room for improvement or determined choice. And again here, in the near future, you have the Eight of Swords, the feeling that whichever way you turn, the odds are stacked.'

'Who were you reading for?' Ray asked.

'Bright boy! I was reading for the killer. I wanted to know what he'd be up to next.'

Ray refrained from asking her if Erica Trimble was mentioned anywhere, but her next words took him by surprise.

'He's done something else,' she said. 'There's another woman here. A Queen of Wands, here in the environment.' She looked at Ray. 'Ah, I've struck a chord there, haven't I?'

'I'm sorry?' Ray tried to deny it but Elspeth waved his objections aside.

'You're a bloody awful liar, you know. Your mouth tightens up, ever so slightly, when you're caught off-kilter. I imagine it would have been less noticeable before you got your scars but it's always been there, I daresay.'

'No one's ever mentioned it before.'

'No, but I'm better than most, remember. Spent my life in close observation of what we term humanity.' Elspeth snorted as though she didn't think much of the subjects of her study. 'Anyway, I think the woman got away, or something went wrong, but here, right here, you've got the Ten of Swords and then the Queen of Swords.'

'Rose's card.'

'That's right.'

'Elspeth, forgive me for asking this, but is this sequence of cards enough to tell you that the killer is coming back? That does seem rather . . . specific.'

'Not on its own, of course. But that's missing the point, isn't it?'

'Is it?'

'Well yes, of course.' She sighed deeply as though he were being very stupid. 'Look, Ray, the cards, the crystal, whatever you use as a tool is only the starting point. It allows the mind to free itself from the everyday constraints we usually apply to our thinking. Lets our intuition, our psychic side come out. And I know, I just know that this is what the cards are telling me.'

Ray thought about it. Intuitive leaps were not something he was unfamiliar with. Often during an investigation he'd reach a conclusion, get a feeling, make a mental leap that the known facts would not have led him to. He'd always put it down to experience, to that unconscious information gathering that the brain does all by itself when the conscious mind isn't looking. Some people might call it 'copper's nose,' and he figured what Sarah termed 'women's intuition' must work on the same level. He strongly suspected too that it was what the so-called forensic psychologists were into, but then, he had a basic prejudice against them, feeling that they were often simply trying to quantify — at great cost — what any copper worth his salt would have been able to tell purely based on their years of experience.

'OK,' he said, 'I'll buy into that theory.'

'Generous of you.' She reminded him again of his beloved Sarah, who could on occasion seem just as brusque. He decided he must introduce the pair of them some time. 'And anyway,' she added in a more conciliatory tone, 'the perpetrator often returns to the scene of the crime, doesn't he?'

As Ray was leaving, he caught sight of the evening papers that had just arrived, piled on the hall table. News of the cards found at the crime scenes had broken.

'*Angels of Death,*' one headline shouted at him and others seemed to have picked up the theme. There were the accusations of a police cover-up that he'd come to see almost inevitable. '*How many attacks on vulnerable elderly women would there have to be,*' one article questioned, '*before the police choose to make the connections public?*'

So, Beckett's gone public, Ray thought. He wondered vaguely what good it would have done for anyone to have known about the cards before. His imagination led him to visualise herds of bouncers trained up especially for the job, frisking visitors for the offending cards.

CHAPTER 18

Alice Weston felt herself besieged. It had begun with one man in a car taking pictures of her house. She'd gone out and asked him what he thought he was doing, only to find that he was from the local paper and would like an interview.

'What about?' Alice had asked him. He had fetched the evening papers from his car.

Barely had Alice recovered from the shock when others had begun to arrive. The local guy, she thought, had been quite nice. Wanting his story but willing to be polite and considerate of her feelings. Later arrivals had not been the same. Cameras pressed against her downstairs windows. People shouting through her letterbox. The neighbours standing in the street, pointing at her house and reading the articles in the papers. When she peered cautiously from her bedroom window, she saw two of them talking to a woman with a microphone and being filmed by a man with an enormous camera. She called Dave Beckett wanting to know what to do, only to be told that he was in a meeting and couldn't be disturbed.

Alice retreated to the rear of her house as far away as possible from the crowd and wished fervently she had listened to DI Beckett and left her home. She'd been interviewed a number of times lately, of course, as part of the publicity drive for the Book of Angels, and she'd coped, just, with the intrusion. But this was different, very different, and Alice was genuinely scared.

There was more hammering on the door, this time from someone who said they were the police. Alice didn't know whether to believe it or not.

She called Beckett again and this time she got through.

'Just sit tight,' he told her. 'I'll sort something out. Can you get out the back way?'

'Only if I climb the dividing wall.'

'Just hang on,' Beckett told her. 'I'll see what I can do and I'll get officers over there to calm things down.'

'I'm not going out the front,' she told him, surprising herself by how panicked she sounded.

'You won't have to, I promise. Look, I'll ring you back in a few minutes and tell you what we're going to do.'

Reluctantly, Alice put the receiver down. She covered her ears against the noise outside and tried to control the tears that pricked her eyelids.

It seemed a long time before Beckett called back. When the phone rang again, Alice nearly leaped out of her skin.

'I'm sending someone in the back way,' Beckett told her. 'A female officer, though she'll be in civvies. Her name's Amy and she's blonde with curly hair and a round face, though she'll kill me for saying that.'

Alice laughed in spite of herself, just grateful of anything to break the tension.

'It'll take them a few more minutes to get in position, but I've a local beat officer talking to your rear neighbours and they're willing to help out, so it won't be long, Alice, I promise you.'

'All right,' she told him, trying to stop her voice from shaking. 'I'll be all right. I was just so scared.'

'I can imagine. Look, Alice, there are officers out front now, get some things together, you might be away for a few days. I think that might be best.'

'Where will I go? I've no one. And if I go to a hotel, they're bound to find me.'

'All right, don't worry, I'll sort that out too. For the moment I'm having you brought to the station and I'll find a place for you to stay — I promise. And, Alice, if you've received any other letters lately, could you bring those too, just in case?'

Alice nodded, forgetting that he couldn't see, but she didn't trust her voice anymore. She crept upstairs, sneaking through her own house and feeling like a thief. Upstairs, she crammed clothes into a holdall paying little attention to what went in, listening all the time for some sound that would tell her that her rescuer had arrived at the back door. Even so, the knock, when it came, had her jumping in shock. She grabbed her holdall and ran downstairs, pausing only to collect her handbag. Outside the back door stood a young woman with tightly curled blonde hair and a reassuring smile. Beckett had been right about the round face, Alice thought absently.

She opened the door and the young woman took her bag. 'All ready? Great. Your neighbours have found a box for us to stand on. I don't know about you, but I could do with being a bit taller.'

She took the keys from Alice, who was trying vainly to lock the door with shaking hands, and locked it for her. 'It's all right now,' she told her gently. 'There's a car waiting in Mitchum Street. No reporters there, no one at all.'

She helped Alice over the wall, keeping up a gentle stream of comforting prattle all the time. Alice barely registered being taken through her neighbour's yard and then their house. She was vaguely aware of the woman she knew only to say good morning to patting her arm and telling her that they'd keep an eye on things while she was gone. Then she was in the car and driving away. Amy touched her hand and gave her a tissue. Bewildered, Alice realised that there were tears streaming uncontrollably down her face.

* * *

What to do with Alice Weston was a problem for Dave Beckett. He thought she might be right about a hotel. She'd been on television and in the local papers — he didn't know about the nationals — promoting her work, so library pictures would be readily available. A safe house could probably be arranged, but that might take some time and he really wanted to go home having been on duty since eight that morning. Thirteen hours so far that day and it showed no signs of letting him go.

He glanced across at Alice, who was sitting in a corner of his office, hugging a cup of tea in her hands like a child with a security blanket. He'd made a promise and didn't want to let her down and, almost absently, he noticed how pretty she was, even with red eyes and tear-stained cheeks. He wondered again why she had never married . . .

On impulse, he called Ray and caught him on his mobile ready to leave Highbury House. 'Do you still have that old cottage of yours?' he asked and explained his problem.

Ray was apologetic. 'I'm sorry, Dave, I've loaned it to a friend, and anyway, Evie Padget would have the news spread to four counties by morning. There's no malice in Evie, but when it comes to keeping secrets, she's no better than a three-year-old.'

He thought for a minute. Beckett sounded tired and a little desperate. 'Just hold on a minute,' he told him. 'I've thought of something.'

Half an hour later, Alice Weston was on her way to stay with John and Maggie Rivers, and Maggie, somewhat bemused at all the fuss but not wanting to accidentally give offence to their house guest, was rooting desperately in her bottomless kitchen drawer, trying to find the Book of Angels she had so unceremoniously stuffed there before Alice Weston arrived.

CHAPTER 19

Elspeth Moore rarely slept well. She often sat up late reading or watching television, and even when she finally did drop off it was not unusual for her to sleep and then wake again an hour or two later. She had grown used to nights of such broken sleep, but this time she had woken with a feeling of unease that could not be shaken.

She slipped out of bed and padded across to her bedroom window. Unlike Rose and Lily, Elspeth had a room at the front of the house, overlooking the London Road, though the view was screened partially by tall trees and a low boundary wall.

Elspeth stiffened. 'Well, I'll be . . .' Despite what she had told Ray, she had not really believed that Rose's attacker would return. Certainly not to come so openly, standing in the glow of the streetlight that illuminated the entrance to Highbury's drive.

Elspeth watched for a moment longer and then she reached for her pink fleece dressing gown, pushed her feet into the men's leather slippers that she favoured and marched off down the stairs, cricket bat in hand. She paused long enough to use the hall phone to call the police, dialling the three nines and squinting out through the stained glass of the front doors, trying to see if her quarry was still there.

'Highbury House, yes,' she told the operator. 'What's the problem? The problem, my dear girl, is that we have a murderer on the loose and he's standing just outside of our front door.'

Impatiently, she slammed the receiver back in the cradle, knowing that the alarms would be set off anyway the moment she opened the big front doors. It would ring in the bedrooms of the duty carers and in Mrs Ellington's room and also at the security company, who should then inform the police. Two calls from the same address, Elspeth figured, were bound to get some kind of response.

She unbolted the doors and stabbed the entry code into the keypad, waited for the buzzer to sound and then shoved her way through. To her great satisfaction, the figure still stood in the cone of light. It turned then, hearing her crunch across the gravel.

'Hey, you there!' Elspeth shouted. 'You just stay where you are.'

For the merest instant, Fly obeyed the order, then ran away from the imposing figure in the pink gown brandishing a cricket bat that she had good reason to fear. But that moment had been long enough.

'My God, you're just a little girl!' Elspeth burst out, and as Fly took off, she gave chase as best she could, pursuing the small blonde figure into Houldich Road and partway down the hill before lack of wind forced her to give up. Elspeth leaned upon her cricket bat and waited until she could breathe again.

'The Knight of Cups,' she whispered. Now that she had seen the would-be killer up so close, the anomalous card made sense.

It took a little while for Elspeth to get back to Highbury. Sheila Ellington and two of the duty staff were on the doorstep, examining the locks and peering anxiously into the night.

'Elspeth! Was it you? What on earth are you doing?'

Elspeth was glancing around. 'No police yet?' she demanded, outraged that they should not have arrived before her.

'Police? No. The alarm went off and the security company called. I told them they'd better report it because I didn't know what had happened. Then we came down and found the front door. Elspeth, you know how our system works, if we have a false call it goes on our record. Too many false calls and no one will come out.'

'This wasn't a false call. The bloody police should have got here by now. I called them on the hall phone before I came out here.'

'You called them? Why? What's been going on?' She drew a deep breath and laid what was meant to be a comforting hand on Elspeth's arm. 'Look, come inside, we'll make a nice pot of tea and . . .'

The arrival of a patrol car interrupted her flow, though, Elspeth noted, it seemed in no hurry and the sirens and lights she felt she had a right to expect were not in evidence. Elspeth strode across to the young officer who was getting out of his car, a puzzled look on his face.

'About time too,' Elspeth scolded him. 'You've missed her anyway. I chased her down onto Houldich Road, but I'm seventy-eight and I can only run *so* fast.'

A second officer had emerged from the car. He was trying hard not to look amused. Not knowing what to make of this old lady in her pink dressing gown, brandishing a cricket bat.

'The murderer,' Elspeth said. 'The murderer was here. I called your lot and then *I* went out to confront her. What I want to know is, where the hell were you?'

CHAPTER 20

The following morning Ray was summoned into the royal presence. Elspeth's phone message had been short and uninformative, just telling him she had new evidence and he must come straight over. Fearing yet another reading, Ray had tried to put her off, but Elspeth was adamant. 'This is different,' she told him. 'I've been talking to the police for hours, useless lot. So I'm in no mood to argue.'

Highbury looked calm and peaceful in the quiet of a sunlit Saturday morning. Some of the frailer members of Highbury's community were dozing in the residents' lounge, others could be seen in the garden enjoying the sun. The twins were waiting for him, though Elspeth was nowhere to be seen. They were twittering with excitement about the previous night's events, and as they gave him coffee Ray learned about the figure Elspeth had seen, how she had given chase and the dressing down that she had given the police when they had arrived.

'A girl?' Ray questioned. 'Is she sure?'

'Of course I'm sure,' said a voice from behind. 'I may be old but I'm certainly not without all my faculties.'

She sat down in the free chair. Rose poured her coffee and handed it across.

'Do you know how long it took those fools to answer a 999 call last night?'

'No, but no doubt you'll enlighten me. Elspeth, what's all this about the killer being a girl?'

'A girl,' Elspeth confirmed. 'A little thing. Quite pretty too, if it wasn't for the silly haircut. Punk or something, I suppose. She looked like a blonde version of that nice television chef. You know the one that cooks brown food.'

Ray shook his head in bewilderment. 'Elspeth, she could have been anyone.'

'That's what your flat-footed friends said. But *I* know better and *you'd* better start listening.'

Ray stared at her, then pulled a notebook from his pocket and fished for a pen. 'All right, tell me. Every single little thing.'

* * *

Fly was in one of her favourite places. She lay on her back high above the noise and bustle of the lunchtime crowds that gathered in the park and gazed up at the sky.

She loved watching the clouds, the birds flying off wherever birds went and the scent of the old roses clambering up the back of the castle wall.

Where she lay had been the foundation for the castle of a much earlier time. Fly lay on the earth motte that had been underpinning for the earliest keep and palisade of Leicester Castle. It was a hidden spot, even though an attempt had been made to add it to the tourist trail that led through Castle Park.

Fly had known this place all her life, long before the rest of the world rediscovered the presence of such a historical structure hidden in plain sight. She had come here often with her mother, and it had become their special place. In those days of intimate childhood it had been like a secret garden, overgrown and private.

Fly much preferred it as it had been back then.

Back in Fly's childhood they'd had to squeeze through a tiny, forgotten gate that never opened fully and clamber up a track that lay almost invisible among the undergrowth and brambles. The flattened summit was carpeted by long grass and wildflowers and stuck through with self-seeded saplings from the birch trees clinging to the steep sides. It was a magical place.

Her mother would sometimes bring a little radio and a picnic, but just as often they would simply lie concealed among the waving feathered grasses and the fresh faces of the ox-eye daisies, and they would talk and dream and forget about the other world where life was not so easy, where Fly was often miserable and just as often scared.

Sometimes, when her mother brought the radio, they would dance together, her mother's skirt brushing the grass and swirling through the flowers.

Fly loved the way it had been back then, before the open gate and the steps leading up the side and the tourist information boards outlining the history of the place. Fly knew about the secret history of that secret time and that was more important, so much more than any illustrated printed sign could tell.

Fly found herself thinking about the woman with the cricket bat and that weird sense of connection she had felt the night before. Fly couldn't really explain why she had gone back, perhaps she had been testing her nerve, perhaps she had been trying to prove to herself that she could do what the old man wanted her to. She had stood there just staring at Highbury House and wondering what to do next when the old woman had come out, the one that had hit her with the cricket bat. And that was so strange too. The way she had felt when she had seen this old figure in her pink dressing gown and leather slippers. She couldn't actually explain what the feeling was except that it was almost a kind of familiarity, as though she had known the woman, mattered to her, had some involvement with her that was more than just being clouted on the knee with a cricket bat. Fly had tried to figure out what had made her feel that way, but she really couldn't.

It was like the first time after her mother had fallen ill that she had met with the old man. Like, but different. The old man had claimed that he was family, and Fly, whose only family had ever been her mother, had wanted to believe him — at least a part of her did.

Part of her had wanted to run like hell. Run as far and as fast as she could go.

Fly thought about the woman again. She had seen her picture in the papers after that first night and learned that her name was Elspeth Moore and that she'd been lying in wait to protect her friend. It didn't say at all how she'd known that Fly would be coming there. It was good though, Fly thought, to have friends, have family, have someone you thought was worth fighting attackers for. She wished fervently that she had someone like Elspeth Moore fighting for *her*.

Fly got up and left the comfort of her place on top of the castle mound. She walked back through the park, turned left and crossed the canal, then strolled across the concourse in front of the university, aware of the fierce heat rising from the pavement, shocking after the cool of the grass and tall trees. Thinking how quiet it was this time of year with all the students gone, she made her way slowly to the hospital, wanting to go and yet deeply reluctant, knowing things would be no better today than they had been yesterday.

The nurse on duty recognised her and smiled in welcome. 'She's just the same, I'm afraid, and there's still no news on when we'll be able to move her to the hospice. But she'll be better just for seeing you.'

Fly nodded her thanks. She rarely spoke — that would invite the woman to have a conversation and Fly wasn't comfortable with conversation. She went through to the side ward, opened the heavy door and looked in on a woman who lay semi-conscious in the green-covered bed.

'Hello, Mam,' Fly said.

CHAPTER 21

It seemed convenient for Ray and Beckett to meet at Maggie's as Alice was still there. The kids and dog were on the rampage as usual and Ray watched them fondly from the kitchen window. He'd never been too keen on children, never really had too many dealings with them before, but he'd become fond of this pair, coming to see them as part of the informal extended family he had gathered about himself in the past three years.

John Rivers breezed in. He was in civvies, Ray noted. John only managed to look like a minister on Sundays when protocol dictated that he dress the part. Other times it was more likely to be jeans and a baggy jumper — or a T-shirt, as now, mired in green mould from the dead tree he had been clearing from the garden.

'Ray, great to see you. And this must be DI Beckett. I've heard all about you.'

Dave Beckett shook his hand. It too was grimy and rather green. Belatedly, John noticed and apologised. 'I've been playing hooky all afternoon. Trying to make some sense of that wilderness. Alice has been helping out, she's a demon with a machete.'

Maggie laughed. 'I think we're finally getting somewhere.'

The large Victorian vicarage came with an equally large Victorian garden and it had had several incumbents since the last competent gardener. It had been something of a trial ever since they moved in, though Ray could now discern a reasonably well-clipped lawn and some flowerbeds emerging from the undergrowth.

'Where is Alice?' he asked.

'Gone upstairs to clean up,' John told them, making do himself with the kitchen tap. 'She'll be down in a minute.'

'She's nice,' Maggie added.

'I'm really grateful to you,' Beckett told her. 'I know it's a big imposition.'

'Oh, it's no bother, and I don't think anyone would think of looking here for the famous Alice Weston. She had to stay out of the way this morning, I had the Ladies' Guild come round and they're a sharp lot. I couldn't risk having her meet them. But she can go out and wander in the garden and no one will see her, and the house is big enough to lose a dozen Alice Westons in without us falling over each other.'

'What about the children? Do you think they'll say anything?'

'They know all about Alice, who she is and so on. But they know not to say anything, and as it happens their best friends are away on holiday for the next two weeks, so we shouldn't have too many outsiders wanting to come and play. After that, it may be a little harder.'

'I hope I'll be back home well before then,' Alice said.

Ray turned and looked at her, interested to at last meet the woman who had illustrated the cards so intricately. She was attractive, he thought, in a quiet way. Her long hair was caught up in a black clip, but he guessed that her usual style was simple, with a fringe, probably as she'd had it since her student days. She wore almost no make-up, just a trace of lipstick, applied and then almost blotted away and a brush of mascara on her lashes, noticeable only because it made them so much darker than her hair.

A pleasant figure was disguised beneath a loose shirt and a pair of faded jeans. She was a woman who, as Ray's mother would have put it, 'could have made more of herself,' and he could not help but wonder if that were because she was comfortable with herself, or because she lacked the confidence to change, to put herself forward.

Maggie had made tea and John arranged a plate of biscuits and little cakes — Ray wondered how long before the children sensed them and came hunting — and the party adjourned to the smaller of the sitting rooms. This was a more comfortable place than the large front parlour that Maggie kept ready for her coffee mornings and official guests. This back room, with its French windows matching those of the dining room, also at the rear, had become their family room, and it was cosily furnished and cheerfully messy.

Ray brought them up to speed on Elspeth Moore's encounter the previous night.

'The local police are passing it off as some old dear feeling the strain and going doolally, if Elspeth's to be believed. I imagine they're taking it more seriously than that, after the attack on Rose, even if they are trying to downplay it publicly. You heard anything, Dave?'

'Nothing official, but Fox did give me a call, purely out of courtesy, and told me what had gone on. Frankly, they don't know what to make of it. I think they'd like to believe it's just a case of overactive imagination on Elspeth's part, and after all, the girl could just have been waiting for someone. I might run if Elspeth came out and surprised me.'

'Waiting for someone. At two thirty in the morning?' Maggie questioned.

'Ah, you lead a sheltered life,' John told her.

'Well, as of this moment, it's all speculation.' Dave Beckett shook his head. 'I'd love to have seen it though,' he added wistfully. 'Fox tells me it's the talk of the canteen. This furious old harridan dressed in pink and wielding a bat like she was about to play for England.'

It was, Ray agreed, an image to contemplate.

'What sort of card would represent a girl like that?' Ray asked Alice. 'Elspeth noticed the Page of Cups turning up when she asked about the murders, but she said that felt off.'

Maggie reached behind the sofa to the sideboard, taking out the Book of Angels pack she had rescued from the depths of the kitchen drawer and laying them on the coffee table in front of Alice. 'Maybe it will help to look at them.'

Alice smiled nervously. She slid the cards from the box and fanned them out face up. 'Cups are usually gentler. But if the girl is young and inexperienced, then maybe . . . You've not given me much to go on.'

'Small, blonde, kills people,' Maggie said. 'That should give a few clues.' She shook her head. 'Sorry, I know this is serious, it just seems so bizarre.'

Alice was thinking, spreading the cards out and examining them. She selected two and laid the Knight of Swords beside the page in the middle of the table.

'One of these, I think. They're both cards of impulse, of actions that are made often before they are thought through, but it depends how old she is, how experienced — oh, a lot of things — and I'm not sure about the colouring. Some people read the swords as redheads. Others don't go in for the description thing at all.' She shrugged apologetically. 'I told you before, I designed them but I'm not a reader. Mostly, I just read the different meanings in as many books as I could find and interpreted them according to those.'

'But you changed some,' Ray said. 'Why did you do that?'

Alice shook her head. 'I couldn't say. Odd things were because the friend I designed them for had her own slant on certain cards. Others . . . I don't know, as I went on I became so immersed in the designs, some just suggested themselves and I couldn't see them any other way.'

Ray said nothing for a few minutes. He thought of the layout that Elspeth had shown him. The Death card crossed by the Page of Cups. Not swords.

'What if you used the Page of Cups? If that were the significator card and not the Knight of Swords.'

'Cups?' Alice wondered. 'Why cups? Cups are watery, emotional cards. The people represented by them are often very loyal, very emotional, attached to family, sometimes a little too eager to please.' She smiled. 'I know more about the cups because, well, according to my friend . . .'

'Your card is the Queen,' Ray guessed.

Alice laughed weakly. 'She says I'm a typical Cancerian. I don't really know about that.'

Ray nodded. 'There's someone I'd like you to meet.'

'Not Miss Moore?' Beckett laughed. 'Can I be there?'

'It's Mrs, actually.'

'You're kidding me. *Mrs* Elspeth Moore? What poor sod was she married to?'

'Rose tells me he was a colonel. Actually, I rather like her.'

'Well, you must have a taste for strong women. Mind you, I've met Sarah. Don't get me wrong, Ray, I think she's an amazing person, but she scares me to death.' He frowned as though something struck him. 'You know, I always thought places like Highbury House were for folk who couldn't look after themselves, who needed, you know, nursing or what-not. Not for women like the Spencers and Elspeth Moore.' He laughed. 'They've certainly opened my eyes.'

'Oh there are enough frail elderly at Highbury,' Ray said. 'Elspeth Moore, I think, was just tired of being alone. The Spencer sisters lost their home when Rose's husband died and left a pile of debt. Lily was living with them at the time, and neither of them, Lily says, could face the thought of trying to start again. They sold up, paid their debts, and their home at Highbury is partly funded by dwindling savings that they are both hoping will last out. I suppose they just thought it was time to be looked after.'

John Rivers was slowly sorting through the cards that Alice had left upon the table.

'What do you make of all this?' Ray asked him. 'Maggie said these belonged to a parishioner who scared herself playing around with them.'

John nodded, he glanced up at Alice and smiled. 'They're beautifully done. They remind me of icons.'

'Funny remark coming from a vicar.'

'Not really. The major cards, as I understand it, are archetypes. Images and concepts that appeal to the oldest part of our unconscious, the part that creates our dreams . . . and our nightmares. You look at these images and you see reflected in them the greatest of our hopes and the greatest of our fears and I think Alice has remembered something in her presentation of these images that most of us like to forget.'

He selected one card and laid it down in front of Ray. It was an image at once disturbing and oddly attractive, Ray thought. A beautiful, armoured man surrounded by a bright halo and blessed with wings but whose expression hardened upon the handsome face and whose eyes glittered with purpose. He held by the arm a struggling man who sank to his knees with the weight of the chains the winged figure piled upon him.

'The Devil. The Angel of Constraint,' Ray said.

John nodded. 'Alice has reminded us that Satan once was Lucifer, the brightest and most beautiful and, oh, the most convincing of them all.'

CHAPTER 22

'How did you meet the Rivers?' Beckett wanted to know when Ray drove him home.

'Hmm, seems unlikely, doesn't it? Me and the vicar. Actually, John knew my aunt.'

'The one that left you the cottage?'

'Yes, he used to lodge with her before they all moved into that great barn of a place. Maggie and the kids didn't move down straight away. Anyway, John and Mathilda hit it off, and when she died, he came to say hello to the person who'd inherited her cottage.'

'They're nice people,' Beckett mused. 'What do you make of Alice?'

'I think she's a nice person too.' Ray glanced sideways at Beckett. 'I get the feeling you think she's more than that.'

Beckett laughed. 'I tried not to make it obvious.'

'You didn't manage it. Oh, it got past me, but our Maggie has an eye for romance, usually even before the pair involved. She said Alice had been talking about you. How nice you'd been and such.'

'Oh?' Beckett tried his best to sound noncommittal.

Ray smiled. 'I told her she should make encouraging noises. That you were single again and that it was about time you put your feet back in the water.'

Beckett laughed. 'What are you these days, the resident agony aunt?'

'It's a hard job, but . . . you know what they say. Seriously though, Dave, I think you should give it a go.'

'I think there might be some small conflict of interest at the moment.'

'Yes, but we'll soon sort that. What's a small blonde murderer between friends?' He frowned and continued more seriously, 'What are the odds on her taking another pop at Rose? Or at Erica Trimble? There's unfinished business there, too.'

'High, I'd have said. Though there's no logic to it. But if Elspeth Moore is right and the stranger hanging about outside Highbury was our killer then we have to chuck logic out of the window and just assume we're after a persistent bastard working to their own agenda. It would help if we knew what that agenda was. Give me a motive like greed or hate or even passion and you can figure out who might have done it nine times in ten. Motiveless crimes are something else.'

'No such thing in my book,' Ray countered. 'There's motives the likes of me and thee can understand and there's motives like . . . like Harrison Lee had when he killed those kids. Random and meaningless and brutal so far as we were concerned. Simply a needful part of his plan to him.'

Beckett nodded thoughtfully.

'Then,' Ray continued, 'there are those who kill so that they can belong in some way. Or because they feel afraid of another person or constrained by them or even encouraged to act in a certain way just to get their approval.'

'What put you in mind of that? The devil image, whatever she called it? Surely you're not taking that seriously, Ray?'

'It was the other way around, really. It started off a train of thought. Like I just said, a sense of belonging. Or a need to belong can cause people to act in some very strange ways.'

'Like the Manson Family.' Beckett laughed, a little embarrassed. 'No, but they do fit into the pattern. So do the gang killings in US cities — some British cities too, sadly.

You want to be a member, you have to kill for the privilege. That the sort of thing you have in mind?'

'Maybe? Or the Wests. No doubt about the fact they fed off one another. Or the boys that killed James Bulger. I don't see one child carrying that through. Not without the support of the other. Failure in the eyes of someone you . . . *respect* is too strong a word in their case . . . feel an association with is often enough of a reason to keep on doing something when everyone else tells you to stop. Look what happened in Nazi Germany.'

'Or Rwanda.'

'Or seventeenth-century Europe.'

'Sorry? I'm missing that one.'

'I was thinking about the witch hunts.'

'Oh. Now you're getting a little esoteric.'

'Or the Spartans and Thebans?'

'Now you really have lost me.'

Ray laughed. 'Teach me to live with an archivist. Apparently their elite forces — their SAS, if you like — were made up of male couples. You fought harder because you didn't want to lose face with your lover . . . or something.'

Beckett was unimpressed. 'I don't think the MOD will be taking that one on board. OK, so you've proved your point. Sometimes people behave more extravagantly because they have someone pushing. Sharing the experience. You think that's happening here? Do you seriously think we're looking for more than one person?'

Ray shrugged. 'I don't know. There's absolutely nothing to say that, is there?'

'No, and what we were saying about extravagance — none of that either. Bethany Himes was killed with a single stab wound. Nothing showy. Nothing more than was absolutely necessary. Of course, it's possible the violence will escalate. It often does.'

'Not always. Look at Harold Shipman, he kept to roughly the same MO all the way through. Just what was necessary, nothing more.'

'Don't even go there,' Beckett said. 'Anyway, Shipman seemed to know what he was doing. Our killer is sometimes inept. Three deaths and two failures.'

'Good! But doesn't it strike you as odd? I mean, Bethany Himes, Cora Hudson and Marilyn Simpson were all killed with a skill and an economy that speaks of someone cool, calm, collected and capable of planning. And it was as up close and personal as you could possibly get. Use of a knife and at very close quarters. Then Rose. The would-be killer climbs through a window and puts up absolutely no defence when they meet resistance.'

'Would you? Faced with Elspeth Moore and her trusty cricket bat? But no, I do take your point. And this last one, Erica Trimble. That makes so little sense. I mean, who walks up to their victim in a garden in broad daylight like that? You'd have to have nerves like Sweeny Todd to make that work, and our boy, girl, whatever certainly didn't.'

'So, two distinct MOs. Two distinct approaches. Two distinct killers?' He glanced at Beckett, who refused to bite. 'And then there's this idea that keeps showing up in the cards, whether we take notice of it or not — the whole matter of constraint.' Ray shrugged again. 'I'm beginning to sound like Elspeth Moore, taking the cards as *prima facie* evidence. My brain's been going in circles so much it feels as though I've been on another of those blasted rollercoasters.'

'Rollercoasters? Who got you on a rollercoaster?'

'Maggie's kids. First and only time.'

Beckett laughed. He was fishing in his pocket. 'I've got something for you to show your ladies. I had it faxed through to me from Erica Trimble.'

Ray glanced at it. It was still light enough in the car to give him some idea of the picture. It showed a young woman dressed in a scanty but frilly costume being hoisted into the air by an elephant.

'Erica Trimble in her young days,' Beckett said. 'On impulse I asked the locals to see if she'd ever been a performer of any sort. Seems she did two years in a circus before settling down.'

'Our link?' Ray asked.

'Who knows, but it's the only possible so far. I've turned up nothing similar on Bethany Himes or Cora Hudson. Yet. I made this copy for you to show the Spencer sisters. Tell them her name used to be Erica Jones.'

CHAPTER 23

Ray had called in at Highbury House on his way home. He was now evidently such a familiar visitor that he was buzzed through without being questioned first. The sisters agreed that Erica Trimble, who had been Erica Jones, looked vaguely familiar but they couldn't place her specifically. Ray promised that he would look through the box of assorted memorabilia they had loaned him and also ask Phil to keep his eyes open for someone who looked like Erica while he was digitising their films for them.

He arrived home a little later than usual to find Nathan there, the red-and-chrome motorbike parked outside. Nathan and Sarah were in the kitchen, Nathan slicing peppers while Sarah stirred something in a pan that smelt rather wonderful. Ray tried to remember if Nathan and Sarah had actually met before, he didn't think they had but they seemed perfectly comfortable with one another. The thought took him by surprise. He'd rarely seen Nathan look comfortable with anybody, Maggie's kids apart.

'I was talking to Sarah about the cottage,' Nathan said. 'I like it there. I think if it's all right with you I'd like to stay. I get on well with Evie, and I get on fine with your ghost. Kitty seems to be quite happy for me to be around. If you could let me know how much the rent would be, and then I can get vegetables planted in the garden.'

For a moment Ray was so taken aback that he just stared at the young man, and then, responding to a glare from Sarah, he nodded. 'So you're aware of Kitty.' He felt oddly put out. He'd had this strange fancy that he was the only one, apart from his late aunt, who could sense this familiar presence. The woman who had lived in the cottage three hundred and fifty-odd years ago.

'I don't think she'll move out now,' Nathan said. 'But she seems happy for me to be there.'

'It's been empty long enough,' Sarah pointed out. 'It's a lovely little place, somebody ought to live there.'

Ray nodded, it did in fact seem like an ideal solution. Nathan handed the chopped peppers to Sarah, who added them to the pan.

'Good, so we can sort out the details later, food will be about five minutes if you want to lay the table and stick the kettle on. What sort of day have you had?'

While they ate Ray brought them both up to speed on his visit with Beckett to see Alice.

'I feel sorry for her,' Ray said. 'She seems to have created quite a monster.'

'Well she can't be held responsible for how somebody else uses her art,' Sarah declared.

'No, of course not, but it must be quite a frightening thing, having your creation interpreted by a murderer.'

Nathan said nothing and seemed focused on eating, though Ray could see he was thinking deeply. As Ray cleared away, he heard Sarah ask Nathan what he thought about the cards.

'Sometimes people don't know what they've created,' Nathan said. 'They take fragments of knowledge from too many different places and fuse them into something else and sometimes those things can argue with one another.'

'A bit like fusion food,' Sarah suggested. 'If the chef knows what they're doing then it can be wonderful. If they don't then I'd much rather have fish and chips.'

Ray laughed but Nathan was nodding thoughtfully as though this was quite a profound idea. Ray set the cheese-board and a bowl of fruit on the table and went back for crackers. It occurred to him suddenly that Nathan was actually quite worried about this strange mix of Alice's.

'This might sound like a stupid question' — he put the crackers on the table and watched as Nathan carefully selected a handful of grapes and laid them out on his plate — 'but do you think she inadvertently created something dangerous?'

Nathan's knife had been poised to cut some cheese, but he laid it aside now as though he needed to focus all his attention on his words. 'Sometimes when you create a new pattern you also create a new reaction to that pattern. There are thousands of different kinds of tarot packs a tarot reader could use. But there is something about the Book of Angels that makes sense to whoever planned the killings. It's as though this person has recognised a pattern and feels it speaking directly to them.'

Ray was puzzled. 'But as you say, there are thousands of different tarot packs and quite a few oracle packs, apparently.' He had done some research on the internet and had been astonished at the variety of objects sold that in some way claimed to foretell the future. If you could read them right.

Nathan nodded and finally selected his cheese, cutting carefully as though this was a serious matter. 'When people have a particular idea, they look for those things that reinforce that idea. They *only* look for things that reinforce that idea. I think when Alice Weston made her pack of cards she accidentally created patterns that this person recognised. She accidentally reinforced an idea that this person already had.'

'And that was enough to start them killing?' Sarah was caught between outrage and a kind of black amusement.

Nathan sliced the cheese that he had on his plate into four precisely equal sections and then shook his head. 'No, I think Ray will agree with me that these are just the latest deaths, that there have been deaths before.'

'Reluctantly, I do agree with you,' Ray said. 'When we find the person responsible, I have no doubt they will have a criminal record and probably a record for murder. This kind of organised thinking, these planned attacks, they don't come out of nowhere. The Book of Angels might have triggered something, maybe even triggered a new wave of violence, but the criminality is already there, the pattern of offending will already be there.'

'And so, are the police looking at previous records? I mean, presumably they are.'

'I'm sure they will be,' Ray assured Sarah. 'Had I been SIO in this enquiry then yes, part of my team would have been looking for previous offenders, but I have to say that attacking elderly residents of care homes is a little unusual. The public perception is that the elderly are always vulnerable. When an elderly person is attacked, of course it hits the headlines, but they're not the most commonly murdered group by any means. That particular honour goes to young men. No, this is an extraordinary set of circumstances and there are very, very few leads.'

'And what do your professional instincts tell you?' Sarah wanted to know.

Ray hesitated. An idea had been nagging at him, one which he had been reluctant to countenance, and which made the most sense of the evidence he had. He had begun to suggest it to Dave Beckett — and had received no response.

'That there are two potential killers,' Nathan said for him. 'One calm and efficient and one who has failed twice. Is that what you're thinking?'

'I'm afraid it is. Two killers, aware of one another, perhaps, and I hate to put it quite this way, but dividing the work between them. Whatever it is they have in mind, whatever plan is at the heart of this — and I have no doubt there is some overall objective — I think there are two of them, and I'm pretty sure Dave Beckett thinks so too. He just doesn't want to say it out loud.'

* * *

112

Fly sat at her mother's bedside, holding her hand. The hand was so bony and fragile, skin paper dry and blue veins standing out. She had never been a heavily built woman, but now she was fragile as a baby bird. It broke Fly's heart to see her like this. Her breathing rasped. It was shallow and uneven, and Fly knew that she could not last much longer.

'Why do you want me to do this, Mam? Why did you send me back to see him? I don't understand. I hated it, Mam. I hate *him*, Mam. I can't do it. I'm scared if I don't try I'll end up dead like them.'

The woman lying in the bed did not move or respond and Fly knew that she'd get no answers here.

A nurse came in, checked the machines that beeped and examined the machines that flashed and smiled at Fly. 'You're here late this evening, love. Have you got someone picking you up? I can phone your Lynn if you want, you know she won't mind coming to get you.'

Fly managed an awkward smile. 'I'm going in a minute. I just wanted to come in and say goodnight.'

'Best sneak out before the nightshift comes on, you know it's past visiting.' She smiled her understanding at Fly, gently patted her shoulder, then left the room, and Fly got up to leave. The mobile phone in her pocket buzzed with an incoming text and she knew it would be Lynn wondering where she had got to and if she was all right. She supposed Lynn was trying to be kind.

She texted her as she walked down the empty hospital corridor telling her half-sister that she was coming back and that she had just called in to see her mum. On one side of the corridor there were windows and the dark outside made mirrors of them. Fly caught sight of her reflection, imperfect in the shadowed glass. A small, slight figure with blonde, close-cropped hair, looking even younger than her fifteen years, what few curves she had hidden by baggy jeans and a loose hoodie. Fly paused and stared at her other self in the glass and then wiped tears from her cheeks and turned away.

CHAPTER 24

Richard Hennessy had once had a comfortable life with a wife and family. He'd been deputy manager at his local bank. He had gardened on the weekends, played the occasional round of golf and enjoyed tinkering with an old car, which he declared was vintage but which his family referred to as 'the banger.' He was an ordinary man — quiet, cheerful, friendly enough, but outside of working hours had preferred to spend time with family. When his wife had fallen ill he'd been heartbroken. He had taken early retirement to nurse her, the children having flown and with families of their own now scattered across the country. Five years later she had died, a longer time than the doctors had initially given her, but it seemed that this precipitated a downward slide. At the age of only sixty-eight, to his children watching him standing in the garden of remembrance it had been obvious that this was now a frail old man.

They had done their best for him, visiting and phoning, but their own children were growing and had demands on their time elsewhere. Each time they saw their father they had noticed further decline, until eventually it became obvious that he could not tell one day from the next, one daughter from the other, and was forgetting to eat and even to drink.

And so he had fetched up here, in this little council-run home, pleasant enough but basic, and though he had seemed bemused by the move, he seemed to settle. Perhaps he did not fully realise where he was.

By the time Richard Hennessy had reached his late seventies, and a decade had passed since his wife died, he was barely recognisable as the good-humoured, quiet man who had been a cheerful father, an efficient deputy manager and a not-terribly-good mechanic. His health was poor and his key worker was increasingly worried that he was struggling to eat and showing less and less interest in life. No one really expected Richard Hennessy to last too much longer, but they certainly did not expect to find him sitting in his chair, looking out of his bedroom window with a knife-wound in his chest, life extinguished, and what they at first took for a playing card tucked into his hand.

Beckett called Ray and told him that there had been another murder, this one as efficient and practised as that of Bethany Himes.

'What card was he holding?' Ray asked.

'The King of Swords.'

'That means . . .' Ray vaguely remembered that Elspeth had used that as his significator.

'Don't bother, I looked it up. Alice kept quite close to the original tarot meaning for the King of Swords. It's usually a man in authority — doctor, lawyer . . . bank manager. Actually, he was deputy manager, but you take my point.'

'So whoever left the card knew quite a bit about him. Like the last times.'

'It looks that way, but as I said before, the meaning of the cards is flexible enough to fit whoever. If they'd left the King of Wands, it might've indicated that he was a good problem-solver, hammering at something until it got done. At least, I think that's what it means. But whatever.'

'True,' Ray agreed. 'But for whoever chose that card and left it, the meaning was undoubtedly clear. They chose that card and they killed him for a particular reason.'

'I'm giving you a heads-up now, the evening news is going to be full of it, and quite understandably so. You might want to get on to your ladies before it breaks. Mitigate the upset as far as you can. I'm going to give Alice a ring.'

'Are you now?' Despite the gravity of the situation Ray could not keep the amusement from his voice. Dave Beckett sounded quite eager to have a reason to phone Alice Weston.

'Leave off, Ray. OK, she's nice, attractive, appealing, all of that. But we need to catch a killer first.'

'So how did the killer get in this time?'

'Now that is a good question. The doors and windows are alarmed, most of the patients at the home have dementia, our victim included, and the home takes security very seriously. Richard Hennessy had a key worker — she'd gone in to get him up and give him his breakfast just after eight. Apparently he liked to have breakfast in his pyjamas and dressing gown and get dressed afterwards. He ate his breakfast sitting at a little table by his window. There's a bird table just outside, and it's a ground-floor room. Someone always put bird food on the table first thing in the morning — he liked to watch them while having breakfast. His key worker — Janice, nice lady — she said he was losing interest in most things but he still liked to watch the birds, so they made sure that there was always food on the table.'

Beckett paused and Ray sensed that something else was bothering him, something saddening him. Beckett continued, 'The staff do their best, but it's a shabby old place. I hope when my time comes I end up somewhere more like Highbury House, that's all I can say. Anyway, apparently his motor control wasn't particularly good, so they made sure everything was cut up into little slices for him — his toast, his bacon — so he could manage them easily. His key worker left at about eight fifteen. When she came back she found him dead. Having talked to the staff, there seems only one way anybody could have got in. The kitchen door was open for a delivery, the outer door was propped open so they could bring the groceries in.' Ray could hear Beckett rifling through

116

notes. 'It's a bit of a complicated system they've got, just let me tell you how they do it. Deliveries are brought into a little lobby area at the rear of the kitchen. The driver pulls the van up close to the outer door, the kitchen staff wedge it open for him and he drops everything off into this small area at the rear. The doors to the kitchen itself are kept shut and the alarm still on while they unload. Apparently there have been a couple of occasions when residents have wandered down to the kitchen, despite the best efforts of staff. Once the driver has finished unloading, he knocks on the kitchen door and un-wedges the outer rear door, closes it behind him, goes on his way. The alarm is then set on the outer door, the kitchen door is opened and the staff bring the boxes through, either into the kitchen or into the storeroom. Now, it might just have been possible for someone to nip in, hide in the cleaning cupboard off the lobby, and then sneak in through the kitchen when the kitchen door was open.'

'Risky,' Ray said. 'How many kitchen staff?'

'At that time of the morning, the cook and one assistant were in the kitchen, the other two assistants were helping serve meals. The cook and helper were in and out of the storeroom, so it could have been done. But as you say, risky.'

'And how did they get out?'

'Just before the body was found, an alarm went off to signal that a fire door had been opened. The fire door opens into a small courtyard area with a high fence around it. If there was a fire then a member of staff would open the gate and lead the residents out into the car park just beyond. The staff were out there in moments and one of the residents was found standing in the garden, having gone out through the fire door, so our best guess is that's the way the killer left. Of course the staff then went to check on all of the other residents, because some were very upset by the alarm going off, and that was when Mr Hennessy was found.'

'And what time did the alarm go off?'

'Five minutes after his key worker left Mr Hennessy. Evidently the killer was waiting, saw her going in with a tray, went in after, single stab wound and gone. It's cold, Ray. Very cold.'

'And what time was the delivery?'

'The driver left at ten minutes to eight, which means that our killer was most likely on the premises for something like half an hour at least.'

'So the driver leaves, the kitchen staff are busy putting things into the storeroom, and there are only two people in there anyway. Our killer comes out from hiding, skips through the kitchen and into the main building. So there's no alarm from the kitchen into the rest of the home?'

'It's separated from the main building by a long corridor, and most of the residents eat their breakfast in their rooms. The key workers find it easier if they're just focusing on one person. Some can manage to eat on their own and others need help, which is why two of the workers in the kitchen assist the care staff. They're often short-handed, apparently. Lunch and dinner are always in the dining room, and at that point, after the meal has been served, the door that leads to the kitchen is alarmed. As I said, the staff are conscientious, but nothing is infallible.'

'Not infallible, no, but it suggests that our killer had intimate knowledge of the organisation.'

'It does indeed. And in the kind of detail that a random visit would not throw up. Perhaps someone who worked there, or someone who visited often enough, or who delivered there.'

'However you look at it,' Ray said, 'another person is dead and the media are going to have a field day.'

* * *

Fly sat with the old man and her half-sister in the conservatory. The television was on and carried the reports of a man murdered in a care home about twenty miles away.

Fly watched impassively. The old man and her sister listened to the report with an intensity that she hated. Lynn was five years older than Fly, and apart from the fact that she too was blonde, they could not have looked more different. Fly's half-sister wore her hair long, she was slender and tall in skin-tight jeans and a white shirt. Her make-up was immaculate and nails carefully manicured.

'You see, Fly, that's the way it should be done,' the old man told her. 'Lynn knows what she's about, you could learn from her.'

One of the staff put her head around the door and asked cheerfully if they'd all like a cup of tea. The old man agreed that he would, Lynn said that she was about to leave and asked Fly if she'd like a lift back to the hospital. Fly reluctantly accepted.

The carer nodded at the television. 'What a terrible business. But don't you worry, Mr Kane, security is being tightened up here. We'll be keeping all of our people safe.' She bustled away, and as Fly stood by the door waiting for Lynn to gather her bag and exchange a last few words with their mentor, she heard the woman say to another member of staff how lovely it was when young people come to visit their elderly relatives, but you'd never know the two of them were sisters, not to look at them.

'Half-sisters, apparently,' her colleague said. 'Different mothers, I think.'

There was nothing unkind in the comments, but Fly felt it keenly that somehow she was considered less than Lynn. Lynn was so obviously glamorous and beautiful and intelligent when she spoke. She was so confident and so capable of pleasing the old man because she was as competent at killing as she was at everything else.

Fly and Lynn walked out of the home together and Lynn unlocked the car. 'Don't take it to heart, some of us find things natural and easy to do, others don't. We're just different, that's all.'

Fly didn't reply. She opened the passenger door and slid inside.

'How's your mum doing?'

'Not good,' Fly admitted. 'They're trying to find her a place in the hospice, but it's taking a while.'

Lynn reached over and patted her hand. 'I know it's tough, lovely, but you are going to have to prepare yourself. You have to let her go and concentrate on the living, on how you are going to cope afterwards — you know that, don't you?'

Fly didn't respond, she didn't trust her voice and the tears were starting. Angrily she swiped them away.

Lynn paused at the exit to the car park, waiting for the traffic to thin.

'How could you do it?' Fly asked her. 'I tried, I just couldn't. He thinks I'm weak.'

'According to the way he thinks, you are.' Lynn cast a sympathetic glance at Fly. 'Look, I'll talk to him again. Remind him that not everybody is cut out for this sort of thing. You're more like *your* mother, I'm more like mine.'

They pulled out into traffic. 'You want me to do it for you?' Lynn asked.

'He'd know.'

'So what? What's he going to do about it? Look, he's got a bee in his bonnet about this, but that doesn't mean you have to have one too. Me, I'm quite happy to go along with it, but you, Fly, you're cut from different cloth. Walk away, no one can blame you.'

'*He* will. Besides, I know too much,' Fly said miserably.

'I trust you to forget what you know. And I'll convince him too.'

Fly shook her head. 'Mam tried to get away from him. He pulled her back, and he made her let him see me. Said I was family, so I had to.'

Lynn tapped on the steering wheel. 'You want some advice? Well, I'm going to give you some whether you want it or not. Your mum is going to die, nothing you can do about that. When that's over and done with, focus on school, focus on your exams, decide what you want to do in the future. And as soon as you can move, you go as far away from here as it's possible to get — just go. There's nothing to keep you here. It's me he wants, it's me he can teach, not you. Fly, you don't belong here, understand that? You go and do your own thing. What's he going to do? He's old. He's finished.'

Fly looked at her half-sister and wondered suddenly how Lynn — so confident, so competent, so beautiful — could be so fucking stupid. 'He don't leave things unfinished, you know that. That man you killed did something years ago, but the old man didn't forget about it, did he? He just stores it up, keeps it in that book of his, that list of people who offended him, that let him down. You think he wouldn't send you out after me if I let him down again?'

Lynn frowned. 'You're overreacting.'

'Am I? And that old woman he sent me to, the one up north. She was younger than you when she pissed him off, but it's still on his list, still unfinished business. He's fucking nuts and you know it. Maybe you are too.'

She saw Lynn's expression change and knew she'd gone too far. Fly mumbled an apology. 'I'm just scared,' she added.

The anger left Lynn's eyes as swiftly as it had arrived and she reached out again to pat Fly gently on the hand. 'It'll be fine,' she said. 'I'll drop you at the hospital. Go see your mum — and don't you worry, I can take care of things. He doesn't care who does it as long as somebody does.'

They drove in silence for the next few minutes and then Lynn pulled into a bus stop close by the hospital.

Fly scrambled out. 'He cares,' she mumbled. She knew for certain what Lynn did not want to admit, that he had to be in control — of everything, no matter how small.

CHAPTER 25

The family of Erica Trimble had taken her away from the sheltered housing scheme, deciding she was no longer safe there. Having heard the news about the death of Richard Hennessy, Erica didn't think that she would be safe anywhere. She'd had a lucky escape, that was certain, but Erica was now deeply troubled for another reason. Her daughter had taken some persuading that she should call the police. She thought her mother was best off out of all of this, that she should not attract more attention to herself. She had told her mother that she would not telephone on her behalf and thought that was the end of the matter. But Erica was perfectly able to use the mobile phone that her children had given her in case of emergency, and an hour later a rather young police officer was sitting drinking tea and listening as Erica Trimble told him that she had known this dead man, this Richard Hennessy.

'We went to the same school,' Erica insisted. 'We lived only a couple of streets away from one another, and when we were all leaving school — it was fifteen in those days, you know — the whole group of us, a whole gang of us still hung around together. There was me, there was Richard, Luke and Eileen, though they are now in Canada of course, childhood sweethearts and . . .'

'I'm sure he doesn't want your family history, Mother.' Erica's daughter turned to the young officer. 'I'm so sorry, I told her not to disturb you. This whole business has played on her mind, of course.'

Erica Trimble turned sternly on her daughter, her face wearing that expression that Clara remembered from childhood. The one that said that there were times when children should be seen and not heard. She began to protest, but her mother had already turned her attention back to the police officer. 'The fact is that Richard Hennessy was in the same sheltered housing where I live. Just for a few months. It quickly became obvious that he could not cope on his own, not even with the help of the warden, so his family moved him. I don't know where he went, he barely recognised me anyway.'

The police officer left shortly after, but a couple of hours later Beckett was calling Ray to tell him that this was the first positive link between any of the victims and would he ask Lily and Rose if they had ever known Richard Hennessy. Erica Trimble did not remember the twins.

'Which is a pity,' Beckett said. 'If we could manage to connect all the victims together then we might have some sense of what the motive is. Always supposing there is one and our killer is not just choosing people at random.'

'Which you're hoping isn't the case,' Ray said. 'Anyway, why am I acting as go-between, are you that short of lowly constables to send?'

'You know the answer to that one as well as I do. DI Fox is keeping me in the loop out of courtesy, but he doesn't want me rooting around in his territory. And your ladies definitely fall within his purview.'

'Not that he's been in touch with them at all. Everything we know has come through you,' Ray grumbled.

'But that might be about to change. Major Crimes are taking over. The task force has already been put together and yours truly is on the team.'

'You don't sound too pleased about it.'

'As is Fox.'

'And the two of you don't get along,' Ray laughed. 'OK, I'll go and see Rose and Lily later today. And no sense that this latest victim might have made enemies in his life?'

'Everybody that's been interviewed agrees that Richard Hennessy was a nice man, did his job, went home to his family, lived quietly.'

Ray could hear the frustration in his friend's voice and he sympathised. There was nothing more frustrating than a mass of incidents with no obvious connection. 'One thing I'm curious about . . .'

'Just the one?'

'So far the killer has used kings and queens as significators, so that's eight possible victims, unless they decide to use the same card twice, of course. Does this mean that there *are* only eight possible victims? What if the killer also has pages and knights in mind? They can be significator cards as well.'

'Don't even think about it, don't even ask the question,' Beckett told him.

* * *

Ray had telephoned Highbury House and spoken to Rose and Lily, but he felt that he should go and see them on his way home. Sarah happened to be in town that day, doing a shift at what had been the reference library and was now the main lending library, as holiday cover. She met him after work.

'We can leave the car here and walk up, if you like. It's a beautiful evening. Maybe grab a drink and something to eat at the Black Horse before we go home.'

'Sounds like a plan,' Sarah agreed. 'Ray, how worried are you about your ladies?'

Ray shrugged. 'It's more a nagging feeling. If we're right about there being two killers then what if the other one tries this time? They're like chalk and cheese — one cool, calm and efficient and the other, well, happily inept so far. Which raises questions, so many questions. Sarah, I think what really worries me is that I can't get my head around what is going on here. And I know Beckett feels the same, and even though they now have a Major Crimes task force there seem to be no obvious leads, no obvious motives, and if they are dealing with two different people, are they even connected?'

'Well it would be a bit of a coincidence to have two people trying to kill the elderly and leaving these tarot card things behind.'

'Oh, I agree. But what if somehow or other that information about the card leaked? What if we have a simple case of a copycat?'

'I like your definition of simple,' Sarah told him. 'No, there will be a pattern here, it will emerge, and you and Dave Beckett will make sense of it. They've already found a connection between two of the victims — there must be others.'

'Erica Trimble and Richard Hennessy happened to grow up in the same town and they happen to know one another, and yes that is something. But there doesn't seem to be any connection between either of them and Lily or Rose Spencer, the second murder victim, Bethany Himes — or rather the first in this sequence. And then there's the cold case to think about. There's certainly no record of her riding elephants, performing on stage or working in a bank. No geographical link either, and that's the other thing: killers usually kill in areas that they are familiar with, these are scattered all over the place.'

'But you know as well as anyone, geographical profiling is not an exact science and often the evidence for it doesn't fall into place until afterwards, when the investigation can look at the crimes as a whole and understand the killer's daily habits.'

Ray nodded. Of course she was right.

'You're just frustrated because you're on the outside,' Sarah told him. 'A few years ago, you'd have been in that sweaty office, griping and complaining along with all your colleagues and staying till midnight to chase down some obscure little detail and you'd have been happy as Larry. You're just frustrated because Beckett is feeding you what crumbs he can and you're shut out from the rest of it.'

He laughed; she was probably right again.

London Road was dusty, the traffic heavy at this time of night, and he found himself wishing they had walked the longer way through the park. Past the traffic island the cars still queued, but the road widened as shops and businesses gave way to imposing residential buildings. This long, broad section of the road was lined with trees, which cooled the air and trapped some of the dust.

Lily must have been watching through the window, expecting Ray's arrival, because she was at the door when they crossed the car park at the front of Highbury House.

'You must be Sarah. We've heard so much about you, come along inside. Elspeth has been reading for us.'

Despite her enthusiastic greeting, Ray could see that she was deeply troubled.

Sarah had obviously noticed this as well. 'And what bad news has Elspeth found?' she asked.

Lily's hands fluttered nervously as though Sarah's directness had caught her off guard. 'She thinks there's been another death. Not the man, not the King of Swords, we know all about him. This is another queen. The Queen of Wands.'

Sarah looked curiously at Ray. 'Ray, what card . . .'

Ray felt foolish but was nevertheless driven by an anxiety he could not quite justify. 'Go with Lily, I just want to give Beckett a ring.' He tried to smile reassuringly, feeling the scars on his left side pull with the effort.

But Lily was not so easily shifted off track. 'You know about the Queen of Staves. Oh my goodness, you mean Elspeth is right.'

A few moments later Ray was connected to Beckett. Their worst fears were confirmed. Erica Trimble was dead.

'She was still at her daughter's place,' Beckett said, 'sitting in the garden just like she was the last time. But this time

126

the killer didn't hesitate or panic. She's dead, Ray, less than an hour ago, and the killer left the Queen of Staves behind.'

* * *

A few hundred yards from the house of Erica Trimble's daughter Lynn sat in her car and watched the action. No one paid her any attention — just a young woman sitting in the passenger seat of a car, as though waiting for the driver to return. Lynn had found she attracted less notice that way — a driver sitting in one place for a length of time seemed to signal something unusual. A passenger was merely that, someone without control.

It's all about perceived power, the old man had told her, *even in the smallest detail. People are programmed to notice who's in charge, it's a survival skill our ancestors must have bred into us. Who do I avoid, from whom is it wise to seek approval?*

Obviously, she thought, he saw himself very much in that role.

Lynn watched as police cars arrived. The road was cordoned off, and the scientific support van passed her by. She was sufficiently far down the street that she attracted no attention, not even from the neighbours who drifted out to their front gates to gawp.

Lynn thought about Fly. Her little sister Felicity — God, no wonder she never used her real name — would never match up to *his* expectations, this old man who claimed to be grandfather to them both. *Great-grandfather, more like,* Lynn thought bitterly. He had to be about a million years old. And Lynn's father — Fly's father too — had never claimed he was any blood relation.

Did that matter? Lynn didn't suppose it did. This old man had controlled their lives, one way or another, since forever, even before they'd known he existed, because he had controlled their parents with an iron rod, building their dependency and their debt and eventually claiming their children as his own.

* * *

'So, what happened?' Sarah demanded. She was seated between Lily and Rose on one of the large sofas in the rear lounge. Elspeth sat opposite, the cards laid out on a small table in-between.

Ray drew up a chair. 'Erica Trimble had gone to stay with her daughter. Unfortunately, that didn't make her safe.'

'Oh my goodness.' Lily looked shocked. 'Ray, what should we do? They'll come back for Rose, won't they?'

'Dave Beckett is arranging for a police presence here.'

'And what good will that do?'

Ray was possessed of the sudden, inappropriate urge to tell them he'd be sure the constables were armed with cricket bats, but he restrained it, recognised the levity as a symptom of his own anxiety.

'We must go away,' Rose told him. 'Somewhere no one will suspect.'

Ray wondered if the Rivers family might be up to coping with another couple of guests. Three guests, probably — he couldn't see Elspeth Moore being willingly left behind, especially if she found out that Alice Weston, creator of the Book of Angels, might be available to quiz.

He dismissed the idea. But Rose was probably correct. They might be safer elsewhere. 'Beckett may be able to arrange a safe house. But until then I imagine there'll be a constable here and extra patrols.'

'Is that enough? What does Mrs Ellington say?'

The owner of Highbury House had been informed and she was not happy at all. Ray had left her arguing with DI Fox about what constituted adequate provision.

'I could be bait,' Rose said. 'To draw out the killer.'

'Emphatically not,' Ray told her. 'Rose, no one is taking risks with anyone.'

'What do the cards say?'

Ray was on the point of saying 'Damn the cards,' but he was, it seemed, in the minority. Even Sarah looked interested. He noticed that other Highbury residents had drifted over, some standing behind the sofa, one or two propped on

Zimmer frames. Others had brought chairs and were obviously waiting for Elspeth to do her stuff.

Ray sighed and gave in to the inevitable.

'Elspeth,' Sarah asked, 'do you have any sense of how the killer is using the cards? To make decisions, I mean.'

It wasn't a bad question, Ray conceded, and then kicked himself for not having asked it.

Elspeth looked keenly at his partner. 'That's something we've all been wondering. That's what led me to believe that another killing had taken place. I mean to say, it was inevitable that he'd have another go. This is not an individual who likes to be thwarted in his purpose, but I didn't expect the conclusion to be so clear or so rapid.'

Ray noticed that Elspeth said 'he' despite knowing that the one who had tried to kill Rose was a girl. He said so.

Elspeth drew in a long, deep breath. 'There's a man behind this, you mark my words. That little slip of a thing didn't decide to do this all on her own. Either the other killer is male, or there is a man behind this whole appalling proposal.'

'You're looking at three people,' Ray said. 'Elspeth, have you any idea how unlikely that is?' He reminded himself that it was not public knowledge, even at the level of speculation, that two killers were involved. It was something even Dave Beckett had not openly admitted, even with Ray.

'Three people indeed.' Elspeth looked at him meaningfully. 'I might be an old woman and a civilian, Ray, but even I know about modus operandi and signatures. There is one killer who is cold and kills with efficiency and, one would imagine, very little conscience. Then there is our little girl. I don't know anything about her except that I feel she is in up to her neck and drowning. And then there is whoever has planned this, whoever wants people dead.'

'But why should there be a third person?' Ray argued. 'I'll go along with you about the two killers, or would-be killers, but one could be controlling the other. There's nothing to suggest . . .'

'There is a third person at the back of this,' Elspeth said in a tone that would brook no argument. 'Ray, I know you don't believe in the cards, I know you don't believe in my abilities, but there will be a third person discovered. You mark my words. Someone older, more experienced — I hesitate to say *wiser*, but certainly more knowledgeable about these things. Someone who has killed in the past and is now, I think, controlling these two.'

Ray shook his head. What she was saying did make a kind of sense, but there was absolutely no evidence to support it. It was bad enough that you might have two potential killers on the loose, but a third? No. That was an uncomfortable thought.

'I have been attempting to understand what this third person knows, thinks and wants done,' Elspeth said.

'Is this what you were doing here?' Sarah indicated the layout on the table.

'It is indeed, my dear. Now look. You see, I have no idea what significator I might use for the person behind all of this, so I used this fellow here. The King of the World. He would be like the Emperor in an ordinary tarot pack.'

Ray looked to the image of a man on a throne, holding a sceptre and a globe and with a sword across his knees. He was looking out at the viewer, his expression stern and worldly. *A man used to getting his own way*, Ray thought.

'You don't often say no to the King of the World and get away with it,' Elspeth said. She drew another card and crossed the first. 'The Teacher.'

This time a winged figure with children at his feet — books, scrolls and a pen tumbled from his lap.

'This is how he sees himself. It's a perverted version of the truth, of course. What he actually is . . .' she laid another card, this time at the base, below the King of the World. The familiar figure of the Constraining Angel.

Ray found that he was holding his breath. He frowned, suddenly feeling ridiculous. He didn't believe in all this. Elspeth was reading into the cards what she wanted them to say, but the fact was, this did make a kind of sense.

He noticed that she was using a different layout this time, setting the cards down in an almost linear fashion as though she was creating a narrative.

'We have the Hanged Man,' she said. 'The time of waiting, of setting everything in place, preparation which is at the one time necessary and frustrating.'

'Is that him or the police?' Sarah asked.

'Sharp girl. Truthfully, m'dear, it could be either. It could be both. Unfortunately, this is followed by the Tower and the Angel of Transformation, and I think in this case it really does mean the Death card.'

So far, Ray noticed, although Elspeth was dealing the cards from a full deck, they had only been Major Arcana. This changed with the next card she laid down.

'The Knight of Cups. Interesting. Our little friend, the little blonde girl. And then . . .' Elspeth breathed a great sigh of relief. 'The Morning Angel. Sun and brightness and a way out. A glimpse of light at the end of the tunnel, if you like. There's still one more card to lay.' She set down the Knight of Coins.

'What does that mean?' Sarah asked.

'It probably represents our other killer. Someone young but more experienced and probably more driven by material considerations. There's nothing wrong with liking material things, of course. The certain practicality that comes with such concerns is useful and often essential.' She paused. 'I want to cross this card. Now here is someone new. But no, not completely new. The first time I read the cards for Ray, this figure appeared. The Knight of Swords — now who is that, I wonder?'

That will be Nathan, Ray thought. *What part does he have to play in all of this?*

CHAPTER 26

Fly sat beside her mother's hospital bed. The room seemed unnaturally silent. The machines no longer beeped or flashed, and her mother no longer gasped for breath that only rattled in her chest but seemed to bring no real relief. She looked pale and old, Fly thought. Pale and old and dried out, but no longer in pain. Her face was relaxed and almost calm, and Fly was glad of that.

Only that.

Fly had been crying solidly for the past hour. Her mother had 'passed on,' as the nurses put it, only a short while before she'd arrived. They had 'tidied up' so she could go and sit at the bedside, moving the machinery of life out of the room or out of the way, and asked who they could call to come and be with Fly. She had lied and told them she'd contact her sister, but all she really wanted to do was to sit and look until she was exhausted with crying and drained enough not to feel anything anymore.

'Mam, what am I going to do now?'

She could stay with Lynn. That had already been decided. Her half-sister had a flat, large enough that Fly could rattle around and not even be noticed, half the time. She had no other next of kin — she didn't want to count the old man — and Lynn had told her social services would not be bothered as long as she had somewhere safe to stay. Fly had no idea if that was true or not. Her previous experiences with the care system had decided her that Lynn was the best of two bad options. At least Lynn made sure she was fed and housed and turned up for school on time, and she had even offered to take her shopping for clothes, had Fly been interested in shopping for clothes.

Fly didn't know where Lynn got her money from. She didn't ask and Lynn didn't tell, but Lynn had been generous with her these past few months and on some level Fly was grateful. Grateful and scared all at the same time.

Lynn had also promised that when the time came, she would help Fly arrange her mother's funeral. It would be a tiny funeral, Fly thought. Just her and Lynn and a vicar.

The tears had stopped. She didn't want them to stop, but it seemed like she'd run out. Maybe she just didn't have the energy for any more. Wiping her eyes, she shoved the chair back from the bed, wincing at the noise it made as it scraped the floor. She stumbled out of the ward, barely conscious of the voices that asked if she was OK, if she needed a cup of tea, if her sister was coming for her. Outside the hospital, she called Lynn. She could hear that she was driving and had her phone on speaker.

'Mam's gone.'

'Ah. I'm sorry, chick. You sound rough. Go home, I'll soon be there.'

'Where are you?'

'About an hour away.'

'What were you doing?'

'Taking care of unfinished business,' Lynn told her. 'I'll be with you soon.'

Fly hung up. She knew what that must mean. The woman Fly had been unable to dispatch must now be dead. She thought about the woman with the cricket bat and the other woman Fly had been supposed to kill. She thought about all of that as she walked away and turned her steps towards Lynn's flat. And then she thought about it some more and knew she wasn't ready to go back there yet. She walked through the university campus and then up onto the castle mound and sat there for a long time, not thinking about anything and then thinking about it all and then not wanting to think but just to be numb. Her phone rang. Twice. Lynn left a voicemail, then rang again. Fly let it ring. It was early evening by the time she made her way back down the hill, but she had made up her mind.

An hour later Fly was ringing the front doorbell at Highbury House and demanding to talk to the old woman with the cricket bat.

CHAPTER 27

'It's not every day you get a killer knocking at the door and asking for you by name.' Elspeth Moore seemed to be quite enjoying the experience.

'She didn't know your name, she asked for the old woman with the bat,' Rose objected.

'It amounts to the same thing. What will happen to her?'

'She's being questioned,' Ray said. 'What happens next depends on her answers. But Dave will let us know what's going on in due course.'

'She's only a slip of a thing, I can hardly believe it,' Rose said.

'Will the police be staying here?' Lily asked. 'A constable was still stationed on the door.'

'For a while, to keep the media at bay. This is going to be quite a big story. And a complicated one, I think.'

He took his leave shortly after and made his way home. He'd promised to go and collect Sarah as soon as she called him.

There had been half an hour of pandemonium after that ring on the doorbell, when Fly had suddenly appeared and demanded to see the woman who had kneecapped her. Mrs Ellington had immediately summoned the police, but

Elspeth, hearing the racket and with an unerring sense for the dramatic, had appeared in the lounge doorway and confronted the tiny figure.

'You! And what are you doing back here?'

'Come to see you. I need help.'

'Help? I'm not sure I understand.'

Ray, who had followed the redoubtable cricketer out into the hall, had been pretty certain that Fly was now regretting her impulse and was about to run. 'Maybe there's a place we could adjourn to. Rather than involve everyone in the fuss.'

Ray had immediately called Dave Beckett while Mrs Ellington, somewhat reluctantly, showed them all into her office. It felt somewhat crowded with Elspeth, the young woman who called herself Fly, Ray and Sarah all crammed in together.

'So, my dear,' Elspeth had said. 'First you come and try to kill my friend and then you turn up asking for my help. This is a rum to-do, isn't it?'

Fly had stared at her as though she'd spoken a foreign language. 'My mam just died in hospital. I got scared. I know what he wants me to do and Lynn said I should go home and wait for her, but I don't want to go back there. Lynn and him, they'll make me . . .'

'Make you what?' Sarah had asked. She'd sat down next to Fly and rummaged in her pocket for a tissue. 'You look like you've been crying.' She had handed Fly the tissue and then, to Ray's surprise — and Fly's too — slid an arm around the girl's shoulders. It had been too much for Fly. The tears had returned, streaming down an already red and swollen face. She had still been sobbing on Sarah's shoulder when the police had arrived, sirens blaring and blue lights flashing. DI Fox, Beckett in tow, had shown up a few minutes after.

'She's not your killer,' Elspeth had told DI Fox stoutly as he'd edged into the room. 'The poor girl's just spent the afternoon saying goodbye to her mother. She's been in the hospital, so she has an alibi.'

But she was still the one who had broken into Highbury House and had clearly intended to kill Lily. There was no getting away from that.

'She'll need an appropriate adult,' Sarah had said. 'I'm guessing she's still a juvenile. I'll be coming with her until you sort out someone qualified.'

Few people, Ray had thought, ever argued for long with Sarah. Beckett had managed to persuade Fox and off they went — Fly and Sarah in the back of a police car, Fox and Beckett following on behind.

It is, as Elspeth said, a 'rum to-do,' Ray thought as he drove out of town and towards the village where he and Sarah now lived.

But if this slip of a kid hadn't been responsible for the deaths of Erica Trimble, Bethany Himes and Richard Hennessey, then who had? And, more importantly, would they go after Lily again?

* * *

Lynn was both unhappy and angry. She had arrived home to find no sign of Fly. In Fly's bedroom, all her bits and pieces were still there, not that the kid owned much, but she had clearly not returned since leaving the hospital.

She called the old man, Duncan Kane, and told him. He was dismissive. 'The kid's upset, she'll have gone off to sulk somewhere. She'll turn up when she's hungry. She doesn't have the nerve to do anything else.'

As far as he was concerned, Lynn thought, that was that. She wasn't so certain. So convinced was Kane that he could get anyone to do anything at any time that the idea that someone should fail him was a strange and unwelcome one. That Fly had failed him was something he still had not fully acknowledged — the kid would get the hang of it in the end or suffer the consequences — that someone could openly disregard or deliberately go against him never seemed to occur. Once upon a time, Lynn supposed that no one would, but he was an old man now. An old man in an old man's skin, living out his life in an old people's home, and the power that he'd once wielded only existed because a few, like Lynn, allowed it to do so. He believed that he was manipulating her when the truth was Lynn was simply learning from him, taking what she needed, no strings attached.

She tried Fly's phone again and left another voicemail, a message from a concerned sister should anyone else hear it. Fly, unlike Lynn, still believed in the old man's power, that he would come after her or send someone after her. That he would have her killed just like he was having these others killed, these people who had in some way offended him. Lynn had begun to suspect he had no contacts left to do the job for him — just her and Fly, which in reality meant just her. And she had no loyalty. Fly was right about one thing though: if she stepped out of line someone would come after her, but it would not be at the old man's behest. Lynn had a very strong sense of her own self-protection.

* * *

The old man had settled himself to watch the evening news, knowing there would be a report about Lynn's most recent escapade. He listened as his fellow residents clucked and cooed and worried, and inside he celebrated, congratulating himself on his latest protégée. Time had not been kind. He had thought himself retired, past it and forgotten until these children had sought him out. Though he had known they would come, after all — he had seen it in the cards.

CHAPTER 28

Fly shifted uneasily in her seat. A woman from social services had arrived. She had been told this was her appropriate adult, but Fly had refused point blank to say anything unless Sarah stayed with her. She had latched on to this rather fierce woman with bright red hair, come very quickly to regard her as a kind of guardian spirit. Sarah was seated calmly on her left-hand side, occasionally taking Fly's hand, sometimes telling her to slow down when her words poured out so fast they tumbled over one another, landing in a confused heap.

The woman from social services was now relegated to sitting in a corner and taking notes. Somebody they called a duty solicitor sat on the other side of Fly and kept advising her not to say anything. *Just reply 'No comment'* had been his advice all the way through. Fly was beyond that. Her mother had died, the only connection she had to anything like normality or love or kindness. The only person who had ever really truly cared for her. What did anything else matter now?

She told them about her mother, she told them about the old man and about Lynn and she told them about the people on his list who he wanted dead and how she had broken into Highbury House and been attacked by Elspeth with her cricket bat and how she had watched the house, seen

Lily and Rose and not known who was who, and on the night panicked in case she got it wrong, and she had not wanted to use the knife anyway.

The policeman interviewing her kept calling her Felicity, even though she had told him she hated it and that Felicity Connors was somebody she never knew. She was just Fly. In the end Sarah told him that Fly had the right to be called by any name that she chose and that it was disrespectful. Felicity, Sarah said, was a dead name, Fly had ceased to use it. The one leading the interview was a man called Fox and Fly had disliked him on sight. The other policeman, the one called Beckett, she'd have preferred it to have been him asking the questions. Sarah clearly knew this Beckett and liked him. He sat in for some of the interview, making the occasional comment, asking for the occasional clarification and every so often leaving the room to act on something Fly had said.

'Why don't you just go and arrest them or something?' Fly had demanded on several occasions. She had told them the address of Lynn's flat and where the old man was, but this Fox man had accepted all of this calmly and done nothing about it so far as Fly could see. In frustration she turned to Sarah. 'Why won't they go and arrest him? Why won't they go and get Lynn?'

The solicitor tried to intervene, to explain that it wasn't as simple as that, but Fly turned her back on him, her focus completely on Sarah.

'Because it's only your word, sweetheart. And because you're telling your story in such a jumble that they can't quite make sense of it.' Sarah's voice was utterly calm and she drew Fly's attention completely so that it felt as though it was only the two of them in the room.

'I'm telling it the best I can. I don't know what else to say. He has a book, he has a list, he has all of this newspaper stuff. If they go there, they'll find it. He's killed people and now he wants us to kill people and Lynn likes doing it.'

'How did you get to know this man?' Sarah asked. It was a question DI Fox had asked in several different formats and he looked annoyed now, as though his authority was being undermined. But he hadn't adopted the gentle tone Sarah had. Fly wriggled impatiently but Sarah took her hand again, calming her down. 'When was the first time you remember meeting him?'

Fly took deep breaths. Her solicitor — she still could not remember his name — was busy advising her to say nothing, but it was Sarah who held Fly's attention. 'I was dead little, maybe five, my mum met me out of school and said we were going to meet someone, someone who had been a friend of my dad's. We got on the bus and went to this big house. I don't know where it was, but it was a long bus drive and I was really tired. When we got there, there were lots of people and this old lady gave me ice cream. The old man, he was sitting in a chair in the corner of the room, like he was a king or something. That's what I thought, like a king, and after a bit Mam took my hand and she led me over to him and he put me on his knee and he said, 'How are you, Felicity?' I didn't like it very much, but I said I was all right and he said that I looked like my dad. And then we got on the bus and went home.'

'And who did your mother tell you this was?'

'She said I should think of him like a grandfather and I thought that might be nice, my friends at school had grandparents and they were always giving them pocket money and toys and stuff, but then we didn't see him again for a long time and I kind of forgot about him.'

'And the next time?'

'I must have been about ten or eleven, because I'd just started secondary school and he was there one day when I came home. I could see my mum wasn't happy about it. He was on his own, sitting at the kitchen table, and I . . . I don't know, I got the feeling they'd been arguing about something.'

'And then what happened?'

'I didn't see him again for another long time. Then two years ago my mum got sick. The doctor said it was cancer, that it had come back again. She reckoned it was *his* fault.'

141

'And why did she think that?'

Fly shrugged, not sure it really made sense, even though it was something she had believed so strongly ever since her mum had told her. 'She said it was because she was so scared of him it made her ill, because one day she knew she'd have to send me to see him and she didn't want to. But when she got really ill and had to go into the hospital this girl Lynn, she came to see my mum and she promised that she'd look after me because she was my half-sister.'

'Did you know about her before?'

Fly nodded. 'Mam had pictures of her she showed me, that dad had left behind. Dad was married, or anyway he was with Lynn's mum. He left her to be with my mum and they had me and then he got fed up and went to live with someone else. But I'd met Lynn a few times I think, I don't really remember. Anyway, a bit after that I went to stay at Lynn's flat.

'Mam said I should go and see the old man, that he was family and would look after me and that I should do whatever he told me to because I had to learn to fend for myself.

'I didn't want to, and I didn't like it, and I didn't like him. Though Lynn was always kind to me and when I got things wrong she stood up for me.'

'Like when you broke into Highbury House. That went wrong?'

Fly nodded.

'And the old lady who's just been killed, Bethany Himes, you just threw the card at her and ran away?'

DI Fox intervened. 'This is not your interview, Ms Gordon. Continue like this and I will have to ask you to leave.'

'And if Sarah goes, I'll do like that solicitor says and I won't say nothing to you.'

Sarah touched Fly's hand to focus her attention once more. 'So how did this happen? You can't have just gone to see him and then he asked you to go and kill someone. What happened?'

142

For the first time Fly looked totally at a loss as to how to answer her. She frowned and then reached out and clutched Sarah's arm. 'He scared me. It's like . . . it's like he expected me to do things and he said if I didn't then I'd be sorry. That if I did like he said that . . .' She trailed off.

'Did he threaten you?' Sarah again saw the confusion on Fly's face and rephrased her question. 'Did you feel threatened?'

Fly nodded and there was an emptiness in her eyes that really worried Sarah. 'I think we should take a break, don't you?' she announced to the room in general. The solicitor seconded that and for once Sarah was glad he was there. She had to explain to Fly that she would be taken back down to the receiving area, and that, yes, she would be locked up for a while, but she should eat and she should drink and she should try and sleep and that Sarah would come back soon. She would have to make a proper statement, and answer the police's questions and not Sarah's. Sarah knew she could do it, and she would be there with her.

'You'll be safe here, nobody is going to hurt you,' Sarah reassured her.

'But they'll go and arrest him? They'll go and arrest Lynn?'

Sarah looked at Fox, wondering what to say, but at that moment Beckett came back into the room and announced his presence for the tape. He sat down and pushed and paperwork over for Fox to see and then he leaned across the table towards Fly. 'The papers I've just brought in are search warrants. Do you understand what that is?'

Fly nodded uncertainly.

'Which means that we are going to the flat and the old people's home where Mr Kane lives, and we have the right to search his room and Lynn's flat. Now, can you tell us what we should be looking for, you mentioned notebooks and lists.'

Fly looked relieved. She nodded. 'Lynn's hidden stuff in the flat. It's underneath the floorboards in the bathroom.

He's got a folder that he slides behind the radiator in his room. He's got a knife inside a walking stick and uses that to poke behind the radiator to get things out. You can't put your hand in, it's too narrow.'

'Thank you,' Beckett said. He nodded to Sarah and departed again. Half an hour later Ray was on his way to collect her, and Sarah was feeling as though in leaving Fly at the police station, she had abandoned somebody very vulnerable indeed.

CHAPTER 29

'What do you make of it all?' Ray asked as they drove towards home.

'That she's just a scared kid, and scared kids are made to do things they don't want to do all the time. Look at all the ones that get caught up in drug trafficking, separated from their families or the care system by county lines gangs. Look at Nathan and the other kids Harrison Lee brought up to believe they might be the next Messiah. Nathan survived it, after a fashion, but we both know that there were others who didn't. And intimidation, plain and simple, is happening in families all over the country on a daily basis. It doesn't take much for a kid to be frightened into submission.

'I don't know what hold he had over her, not really, just that he scared her witless. This half-sister of hers, she's a different kettle of fish by all accounts. But that early memory she has, of him sitting in a room full of people like he was some kind of king, what do you think that means?'

'Head of a family, head of a crime syndicate, who knows? But somebody somewhere knows who he is and who he was and the chances are he has a criminal record, though maybe not under the name of Duncan Kane. The man didn't drop down from space. He might be old now, he might have been

145

getting on a bit when Fly first met him, but there will be a trail somewhere from when he was a younger man. It sounds to me, Sarah, as though the cards brought him out of retirement in some way, somehow triggered something.

'There will be background, there will be a paper trail, and the best place to start is with the home he's in. I looked it up, it's a posh place. Takes money to be there. I'd like to know who's paying the bill.'

* * *

John Rivers had a visitor that night, unexpected but welcome, nonetheless. Nathan arrived on his red-and-chrome motorbike just as the Riverses were getting ready for bed.

'It's late,' John told the young man standing at his door.

Nathan looked slightly surprised. He never wore a watch and time didn't seem to mean a great deal to him. He was punctual when he had to be, but otherwise seem to drift through the day. 'I'm sorry. I should go.'

'You wouldn't have come if it wasn't important, come along in. The kids had a wonderful time the other day, it's not often they can persuade another adult to go on as many rollercoasters.'

'I think I liked it,' Nathan said. 'Perhaps we should do it again.'

Maggie, wrapped in a purple dressing gown, came out of the kitchen carrying hot chocolate. 'I knew it must be you when I heard the bike, I've done an extra mug.'

They went through to the little sitting room. Alice Weston was already in there, standing nervously by the French doors, wondering who the visitor was.

Maggie made quick introductions. 'Alice, this is Nathan, a friend of Ray's. Nathan, this is Alice.'

'You made this.' Nathan withdrew a pack of cards from his jacket pocket. 'There are things I need to ask you.'

Alice looked completely puzzled, but when the others sat down, she settled herself on the sofa beside Maggie. 'I designed them and painted them, yes, but I don't really read them. Not well, anyway.'

'It's about the design.' Nathan fanned the cards out on the coffee table, Maggie rescuing mugs just in time. He selected three cards, laid them down. 'I can see tarot cards in all the rest, but these . . . Where'd the ideas come from for these?'

Alice recognised the Wheel of Change, the Constraining Angel and the Angel of Justice. 'Why does it matter?'

'Because I think this is what started it, I think this is where he got his message from.'

'You mean the murderer?' Alice looked horrified. 'But why these, I don't quite understand. They aren't so different from traditional tarot cards. I just changed the designs to suit my friend and altered the names.'

'I mean the person who *planned* the murders,' Nathan said. 'I've been looking at the cards, finding out what I can for Ray. I don't think it's the same thing. The person who planned, the person who did the killing, they are not the same.'

'We should talk to Ray about this,' John said.

Nathan took out his mobile phone and then looked at John. 'Is it too late to ring?'

'I don't think they'll mind.'

A few minutes later Ray told them that Nathan was probably correct. Someone had planned the deaths, for what reason was not yet clear, and most likely someone else — in fact, two someone elses — had been commissioned to carry out the killings.

'So what significance do the cards have?' Ray asked, his voice a little tinny on speakerphone.

'The Wheel of Change replaces the Wheel of Fortune in the traditional pack,' Alice said. 'A lot of people just relate the wheel to changing luck and I wanted to get away from that. To make it more to do with actions and habits, not so much random fortune. It can be read as the deep past, repeating cycles, old memories, things that come back to haunt the

147

present or that we have to change in order to move forward. Otherwise, we're just stuck on the wheel.'

Nathan nodded as though this fitted with his own interpretation.

'One card is about revenge . . .'

'No, it's about righting wrongs,' Alice objected.

'If someone is obsessed with being wronged, it will lead to revenge,' Ray agreed. 'Nathan may have put it slightly awkwardly, but I think that's what he means.'

Nathan nodded in agreement.

'And the third, the Constraining Angel, he seems to be coming up rather a lot. I thought he was based on the Devil card in the tarot,' Ray questioned.

'He is, kind of, but as Nathan pointed out I added some of the symbolism. Just little details that I thought my friend might like. In this case it was a kind of in-joke about the boyfriend we both had — I mean, not at the same time, but years ago. It became a kind of joke that he never did his own dirty work, he always got someone else to do it for him. So the little figures in the background, on the long leads, one is pushing the other around because the Constraining Angel told her to. If you look really, really closely you can see one of them has a knife.' She stopped suddenly, put a hand to her mouth. 'It was joke. He used to get people to stab other people in the back — metaphorically, I mean.'

'Not many people would even notice that,' John said. 'I mean, what you do notice is this main winged figure and the smaller figure standing beside him in chains, with the collar around its neck. It looks pretty much like a tarot Devil to me. I've seen a few tarot packs before and that symbolism is common enough. You practically have to get a magnifying glass to see those little figures in the background.'

'Did you tell anybody about this?' Maggie asked.

Alice laughed. 'It's not a secret. I mean, it's not something I talked about much, but there was an interview for a magazine, one of these psychic things, I did it with my friend. People wanted to know what the inspiration was and

I said it was my friend, and we ended up doing this interview together talking about all of the little details in the cards that were personal or quirky. Anybody could have read it. I think it might even be online somewhere. I got a few letters from readers — I don't mean readers of the magazine, I mean readers at fairs and that sort of thing — who got a bit stroppy about what I'd said, that I wasn't taking it seriously enough. And there were one or two said I really shouldn't put personal things into something that was out in the public domain. But it didn't seem to bother most people.'

'People take what they want from the image,' Nathan said. 'People see what they want to see, they always have done and they always will. But I think this spoke to him. It's like it gave him permission. And then somehow the right people came into his life to do what he told them to, and that must have seemed like some kind of magic. Like prophecy. I grew up with people who believed in prophecy, and when they couldn't find the right prophecy, they made one up. When the ideas get fixed, there is nothing you can do about it. Everything they see after that will just confirm what they want.' He paused for a moment. 'Do people often write to you about these?'

'Oh yes, all the time. To be honest, I'm not quite sure what to do with all of the . . . Well, I suppose it's fan mail. I suppose I should be flattered, but actually it makes me feel very uncomfortable. The importance that people attach to these cards, I feel like people are depending on me in some way, people I don't know. I'm not sure what to do with all of this . . . attention. I'm just not used to it.'

'Are any of the letters weird?' Maggie asked. She tapped the cards on the coffee table. 'We only have these because a woman — one of the parishioners — bought them, and she said they were so accurate it scared her. When we talked to her about it, it turned out that the cards seemed to be reflecting a lot of the things that were on her mind.'

'Some people do read them that way,' Alice confirmed. 'They use it like a meditation. It's not that the cards tell you what's happening, it's that, well, this kind of nuanced

149

meaning, which is why I added the two levels of meaning to the book. One is like quick and dirty, for when you want to do a fast reading, the other is for when you really want to think it through. So if you look at a card, like strength for instance, depending on the situation you're in it might be telling you that you have the strength to make it through, or you need to find the strength from somewhere. Or that, if there are other Minor Arcana cards around them, that somebody might be there to have the strength *for* you. You might have the same layout and get three or four different meanings, depending on what people need to see. Which I suppose is kind of what Nathan is saying. But that's taking it to extremes, isn't it?'

'Do you have access to these communications?' John asked. 'I suppose the police have them.' He grinned at her. 'I'm asking because I'm a nosy parker, not because I think it might help. I suppose I'm interested in what people get from this experience, what is lacking in conventional religion. I mean I'm pretty open minded, especially as vicars go, but I'm also really curious just on a human level.'

'Oh, goodness, they got forgotten, didn't they? I mean yes, most of the letters, well the police have them. And I let them access the account. I didn't feel really comfortable doing that, these are people's personal thoughts, but I said they could look at recent emails if it helped. DI Beckett said they could get a warrant or something, I don't really know the ins and outs. But when I packed to leave home he asked if I had anything recent, and I did, just a few letters, but I think they just got forgotten in all the rush.'

'You still have them?' John asked.

'John, you are a real curtain-twitcher at times,' Maggie chided him. But she too looked expectant.

Alice didn't quite know what to say. 'In my suitcase.' She looked at Nathan. 'Do you think the killer might have communicated with me? The police thought there was an outside chance, which I've got to admit I find kind of disturbing.'

'It's possible. You never read the cards in public or anything?'

Alice shook her head. 'No. Like I said before, I learned how so I could understand the layouts and how they related to one another, but I don't even use them for meditation. It's not my thing. I didn't make them for me, I made them for someone else. She happened to know someone who told her that these things could be published. I didn't think anything of it, or if I did I assumed that I'd have to pay to get it done, but we put a package together, sent it off, and they said yes. The rest was kind of word of mouth — it grew slowly. A few people were using them at psychics' and mystics' fairs, then there was a festival somewhere, Glastonbury I think, some kind of weekend conference, and one of the stallholders took some and they sold out. A couple of the shops down there cottoned on and started stocking them, and it just kind of grew. After about a year, they were just part of the scenery in those kinds of circles. Then I got an agent, and someone suggested a deal with one of the supermarkets, as a Christmas thing with the gift book. To be honest, I thought it was a bit peculiar, but it did well, and after that they were everywhere.' She frowned as though suddenly uneasy. 'Then I started getting letters from people claiming it was a bad thing for me to be making so much money off it, but to be honest I really make a small amount per pack. It's brought a kind of security — I mean, I have money in the bank for the first time in my life — but I'm never likely to be super rich or anything like that. No, the Book of Angels is a one-off, I won't be doing anything like it again.'

'Could we see the letters?' John said. 'Yes, it is mostly curiosity, but, well, you never know.'

Alice went upstairs to fetch the correspondence that she had brought with her and Maggie made more hot chocolate for anybody who wanted it. There were only five new letters. Two were from women, Alice said, who had sent her things before. She acknowledged them on her website and they always sent the loveliest cards.

Of the letters, one was just a brief note on flower-patterned paper that said the sender had given her sister a pack for her birthday and that she loved them. Of the other two, one was a man who Alice had heard from previously.

'He had financial troubles, and somebody read for him, if I remember right. They seem to have told him that the best thing he could do was sell up, pay his debts and start again, before he was declared bankrupt. I think that's what he did. Anyway, it seemed to work out for him. He writes regularly just to say hello and that the cards changed his life. It wasn't the cards, of course, it was just a friend giving him some decent advice.'

'Sometimes people listen better if an external opinion is brought in,' Nathan said. 'It can be hard to take advice from those closest to us, but the cards can form a kind of buffer between us and the adviser, and that can kind of help.'

'I agree,' John said. 'When people come to me for advice, they're coming to talk to the uniform, to the dog collar. I could give the same advice down the pub and nobody would listen.'

The final letter was not from anyone Alice remembered writing to her previously. It told a long rambling story about a ghost a woman had seen in a National Trust property and how she had gone home and read the cards and found out that it was a woman who had lived there in the sixteenth century. 'I wonder how she worked *that* out,' Alice said.

It continued that she had tried to persuade the National Trust to stock the cards in their shop, but they had refused on the grounds that it wasn't the kind of thing they normally sold. The woman wanted to reassure Alice that she would continue to fight her corner, until the National Trust gave in.

'Goodness,' Alice said.

Nathan, however, had gone back to the two cards and was studying them intently. 'You say that you have received others from the same people?'

Alice nodded. 'The cards are always rather lovely, landscape paintings or photographs, whereas most of the ones I get are either pretty flowers or some sacred sites or other, Glastonbury, Avebury, or random standing stones that kind of thing. Lovely too, but more what you'd expect, you know? And they're always signed, from an admirer, from a friend, something of that sort. I mean, that's a bit odd, but I've never much thought about it. I've had much stranger ones.' She yawned and then excused herself. 'Sorry, way past my usual bedtime.'

'I should go now,' Nathan said. 'May I take these? I'll give them to Ray and he can give them to DI Beckett, but I would like to look first.'

Alice looked a little doubtful but shrugged. 'I can't see the harm.'

Nathan left shortly after, the motorbike loud in the still night.

'He saw something.' John sounded a little miffed that Nathan hadn't shared. 'Now, what did he see?'

'Whatever it was,' Maggie declared, 'we can worry about it tomorrow. Anyway, Nathan always sees things that other people never can. That's what makes him Nathan.'

Upstairs in the guest bedroom Alice watched the red-and-chrome machine as it disappeared around the bend. She too wondered what it was this strange young man had noticed. The truth was, those very ordinary messages, from the admirer, from the friend, cards with beautiful landscapes or black-and-white photographs, had always bothered her and yet she could never have explained why. It was almost a relief that someone else felt the same way.

* * *

Two search teams had gone out, one to Lynn's flat and one to the home in which Duncan Kane resided. Dave Beckett led this second team.

Because the residents were vulnerable, they had arrived quietly and explained the situation to the home's night manager. Reluctantly, she allowed Beckett and his team entry and led them to Duncan Kane's room. She knocked on the door. 'Mr Kane? Mr Kane, I need to speak to you.'

A few moments later the door opened and a man with thinning grey hair, stooped shoulders and dark blue pyjamas stared out at them.

Beckett showed his ID. 'Police. Mr Kane, I have a warrant to search your accommodation. If you'd please go with my officers—'

'Search my what? What is all this?' He looked accusingly at the manager.

'I'm sorry, Mr Kane, but I can't keep the police out.'

He began to close his door. Beckett blocked him and stepped inside the room. 'Mr Kane, let's do this in a civilised manner. Accusations have been made and I am going to search your room. I have a warrant. If you go with my officers then they will allow you to phone your solicitor, or a family member, or anyone else you'd like to be with you, but the search is going ahead now, so if you'll please leave.'

'If that is the case, then I have the right to be present,' Kane said.

Beckett raised an eyebrow and then nodded. He crossed the room to where a wooden chair was set beside the desk and put it down in the corner. 'Please sit down. You may watch, but you may not interfere.'

The manager was beginning to protest, demanding that they stop now, this was unreasonable, that Mr Kane was an old man and should not be put through this. 'Would you like me to call your family, your granddaughter, someone else?'

Kane glowered and shook his head. He reached for his dressing gown which hung behind the door. Beckett checked the pockets before giving it to him. Then Beckett made a bee-line for the radiator and for the walking stick propped against it. With gloved hands he twisted the top and withdrew the sword, what Fly had referred to as the knife hidden inside. 'A sword-stick. And it looks like an old one, Victorian maybe, not one of your reproductions.'

The manager was somewhat taken aback. 'Mr Kane! You really should not have a thing like that in here.'

Beckett slid the sword behind the radiator. There was definitely something there. It took him a couple of attempts to hook the folder and pull it free. It was old and faded and more of a leather document case than a folder. He glanced at Kane who sat impassive, watching him.

'Some things need to be kept private,' Kane said. 'I don't trust the cleaning staff.'

Beckett opened the case and took out two notebooks and various loose sheets of paper. There was also a large brown envelope, which on investigation contained photographs and newspaper clippings. 'What are these, Mr Kane?'

'Memories. We all like to keep our memories close.'

CHAPTER 30

It had been a long night. Beckett decided that Ray deserved an early morning visit and so he called in, hoping for breakfast. Sarah was making coffee; Ray was cooking eggs. Sarah took one look at Beckett and decided that extra toast might be needed, and a few minutes later Beckett was sitting down to hot tea, eggs, bacon and toast. No one asked him anything until he'd finished eating, for which he was very grateful.

'No sleep then?' Ray said.

'I should be so lucky. Sarah, is there any chance of you coming to be with Felicity . . . with Fly? I know Fox wants to continue the interviews this morning, and she is absolutely refusing point blank to say anything unless you're there.'

'I'm supposed to be at work, but I'll phone in. I still have some holiday left. How is she this morning?'

'I've not seen her yet; I've been somewhat tied up elsewhere. We got search warrants late last night, decided not to waste any time just in case. The half-sister, Lynn Maxwell, she wasn't at the flat, but the drug squad are there now and having rather a nice time taking up the floorboards. I went to visit Mr Kane. He's in custody, pending interview.'

'What will the charge be?'

'Initially it's likely to be accessory to murder, but we'll see what develops. Fly was right about his lists and his notebooks. It's going to take some time to go through everything, and probably quite a while to figure out who this man actually is, but he certainly has a list and crossed off that list are Marilyn Simpson, Cora Hudson, Bethany Himes, Erica Trimble and Richard Hennessy. Rose Spencer and half a dozen more are also named. It seems the man was not averse to using the same card twice — he has significators marked against each one, so there's not much doubt in our mind that he's behind these murders. But of course we have to prove that. For all we know he could be making a list of names, people he once knew, matching them up with significant cards, just for a hobby.'

'And the connection between them?'

'There is no specific connection between any of the victims, from the look of it. Sarah, could I help myself to more tea? It's likely they all have a loose connection to him, though exactly what it is, beyond the fact that they've upset him in some way, is not precisely clear. But we found other things too: he has quite a collection of newspaper clippings. Innocent in itself, but most of them seem to be unsolved murders, dating back four or five decades or more.'

'You think he's a serial killer or something?' Sarah asked.

'Or something. Unless he just likes collecting newspaper clippings.' Beckett sighed. 'He's a strange one, very ordinary to look at, but there's something about him, or maybe I'm being influenced by what Fly had to say.

'Anyway, he'll be interviewed today, and then the evidence will be presented to the CPS, and they'll let us know if we've reached the threshold for charging him, and what with. I suspect we'll start with accessory, see what emerges from there. So that's one thrust of the investigation, another is finding out exactly who this man is. Now we have his fingerprints that shouldn't be too difficult — that is, of course, if he's been charged before. It's possible he's been under the radar all this time. That would be annoying, to say the least.

'Other bits and pieces turned up in his room, more newspaper cuttings and a couple of diaries and some photographs, but exactly how all of this hangs together probably won't become clear until we discover who he is and what he might have been getting up to before he ended up in the old folks' home.'

'I did wonder who was paying for it,' Ray said. 'It's not your standard local authority home, that's for sure. I had a poke around on the website and it's not a cheap place to stay.'

'That crossed my mind as well,' Beckett told him. 'It seems to be financed through a trust fund owned by some investment company or other. I'm leaving someone else to chase that down, forensic accounting not being my area of expertise. It could be as simple as him having paid into some kind of pension scheme all these years, a bit like your ladies at Highbury House did, but somehow I doubt it.'

'And what about the girl? The half-sister or whatever she is?'

'Who knows, she's out there somewhere. Question is, does she want to finish what she started, and does she blame Fly for suddenly finding herself homeless.'

'Well, she can't get to Fly, that's something,' Sarah said. 'And what are you going to do with her, anyway? You can't keep her locked in a police cell.'

'She'll probably be charged later today, then remanded and sent to a young offenders' centre somewhere. She's still a juvenile — fifteen, apparently.'

'So young,' Sarah said. 'How did she get into all of this? I mean, she gave a kind of explanation, I suppose, but it still doesn't tell us what hold this man had on her or her mother. Though I suppose it could be as simple as not having had any kind of counter-voice, nowhere else to turn to.'

'We've tracked down her school and home records now. She was in care briefly. Her mother had cancer, was treated, went into remission, but it seems to have come back two years ago. It looks like her mother brought her up on her own and there's nothing much in the way of a support system.

School says she's an average student, doesn't make friends easily and can be difficult.'

'Looks like she was an easy target for manipulation.'

'She's still not innocent, Sarah, she broke into Highbury House. It was only lack of nerve and the cricket-bat-wielding friend that saved Rose, nothing else. She should be thankful to Elspeth Moore for keeping her from making an even bigger mistake. She could easily have been facing a murder charge just now.'

Sarah pursed her lips but did not argue. 'I'll go and phone work. Then I'll get myself ready to go. Oh, and Nathan called last night, seems to think he's got some sense of how the cards influenced your Mr Kane. It's all very psychological and esoteric but you might want to listen, it might give you some insights you can use if he's right.'

'Nathan?' Beckett questioned. 'I thought you'd lost contact with Nathan.' He looked accusingly at Ray.

'I had. Look, I know you suspect there's more to Nathan than meets the eye and you still have questions about the Harrison Lee business and all that, but you know as well as I do that Nathan is not guilty of anything more than being a little weird.'

Beckett frowned but let it pass. Sarah mouthed 'Sorry' to Ray. She had completely forgotten that Beckett still viewed Nathan with some suspicion and that as far as he was concerned he'd fallen off the radar. Ten minutes later she and Beckett drove away and Ray, having decided to call at Highbury House on his own way into work, left only moments later.

If he noticed a small red car following him, he paid it no attention. Lynn, on the other hand, was concerned with where Ray Flowers might be going to next and just how involved he was with this business. Ray might not be on Kane's list but he was certainly involved with at least one of those who was, and very much involved with the police investigation too from the look of things, and Lynn was not about to leave her task unfinished.

CHAPTER 31

Ray's immediate plans to visit Highbury House were put on hold. Work beckoned — an unexpected visit with his business partner to a client who was interested in expanding his security.

Phil had already left the office on another job but had left Ray a message. He thought he had spotted a young Erica Trimble among a group of people standing outside what looked like an end-of-pier theatre.

Ray took a hand lens and examined the images closely. Lily and Rose stood in the front row, arm in arm and clearly recognisable despite the passing years. The woman Phil thought might be Erica Trimble was two rows back, and Ray agreed, it definitely looked like the woman who had ridden the elephant in the circus all those years ago.

The group looked happy, optimistic — a dozen or so young people and a few older. He guessed they were all performers or in some other way associated with theatre. The sun shone and the sky was blue, on this day a lifetime ago. He wondered if any of the other victims might be in the photograph, if that was even likely. He wondered where they all were now.

Before leaving the office Ray emailed a copy of the image to Beckett with a quick note of explanation. Was it possible,

Ray thought, now Phil had found one of the victims, others might be hidden in this memorabilia?

* * *

Nathan didn't need a great deal of sleep. He napped like a cat when he needed it but was as happy to be awake at night as he was in the daytime. On arriving back at the cottage he had re-examined the cards and letters then left them on the kitchen table till morning. Having snatched a few hours rest he wandered out to the village shop to buy eggs and milk. He liked this morning ritual of going to the shop for his daily needs, exchanging a few words with the owner and then walking back alongside the stream that cut through the middle of the village. He had started to plant the garden and begun to think of this place as home. A new concept for Nathan.

He found himself thinking about Alice Weston and how her life had been turned upside down, what that must feel like. Nathan had rarely felt settled anywhere and so the notion of feeling *unsettled* was a somewhat alien one. He decided that he liked Alice Weston, that she should be added to his loose amalgam of associates and people he almost called friends. He was happiest thinking about them simply as people he liked because Nathan was still not entirely sure what friendship meant. It seemed to mean being concerned about another person and that other person being concerned about you, and within that special group he counted Ray and Sarah, and Maggie and John Rivers and their children. And oddly, the lady who came to clean the cottage, Evie Padget, who spoke fondly of the previous owner and who Nathan sensed was also concerned about him, even though she barely knew him. She fussed, ensuring that he ate, answered his questions about the cottage, told him where he could buy plants and what might grow this year in the garden, what he would have to wait to plant until next year. She told him that Mathilda always had a Christmas tree in the corner of the room, close to the stairs. She told him that he would enjoy going to midnight mass and that nobody minded if he wasn't religious. It's a village thing, like bonfire night and the autumn fair, she told him. Everyone's welcome.

Ray had warned him that Evie was a gossip, but Nathan was quite enjoying that. She didn't seem to expect him to talk very much, but she did like to talk, even while she was cleaning. She explained how the village worked. About who was living where, what children they had, who was worried about their jobs, their lives, their relatives. She talked about her own family, she talked about John Rivers and his family, people who she was clearly fond of. She made Nathan feel as though he was part of a broader social group, and this also was new. Nathan liked it.

Evie was already there when he arrived back for breakfast. She was his first cleaning job in the mornings, twice a week, and her first task was always to put the kettle on, her second to find out what Nathan had been up to and if he had everything he needed. Nathan, in truth, did not need a cleaner. Nathan did not make a mess. But it would have been unthinkable for Evie not to continue to do the job she had been doing for close to two decades. Ray had assured him that he would continue to pay for this service, though Nathan thought he ought to take it over at some point.

'Have you had some letters?' She pointed to the items that Nathan had left on the kitchen table.

'No, they belong to someone else, but she wanted me to look at them. See if I saw anything strange.'

'Oh, indeed, so what might be strange about them?'

'I'm not sure, but something is. Not the others, they make sense, but these two cards, they don't.'

Evie sat down at the table. 'Tea's made, you get on with your breakfast and I'll take a look. Now, what am I looking for?'

Nathan put his bread in the toaster and then set to frying his eggs. Evie picked up the envelopes and examined the postmark, the address. 'Care of some guy in London,' she said. 'You know, it's just as easy to set up a post office box these days as to send things care of somebody. If your friend wants to know how, I can tell them. Good-quality envelopes here, but of course they'd be bought with the cards, wouldn't they? I do like good-quality stationery, don't you? One with a Birmingham postmark, one somewhere else that I can't read, looks like Manchester. Now that's strange don't you think? People usually post letters where they live, and if these are from the same person, which I think they are . . .' She looked at Nathan curiously.

'The handwriting is different. At least, I think the hand-writing is different. Evie, do you think . . .'

'No, dear, this is the same person all right. For some reason they've been trying to look as though it's a different person, which I suppose is why they posted it from a different place, but you look at it careful, like. Both of them say 'regards,' don't they, and on the 'g,' they've tried not to make the loop on this one. They've tried to make it look different, but then they've kind of stopped suddenly, like they've had to really restrain themselves. Look at the pressure on the handwriting, it's really similar.'

Nathan buttered his toast and then popped the eggs on top before he sat down opposite. Evie took charge of the teapot. What she had said tallied with what he had already thought. At first glance it looked as though the cards were from two separate people, but he had already come to the conclusion that it was one person, simply disguising the handwriting. Now why would anyone do that, especially when the messages were so bland? One merely said, *I'm keeping up the good work, hope you are too. Regards, your admirer.* The other was, *Still learning from your wonderful cards, regards, as always.*

'Man or woman?' Nathan mused.

Evie added sugar to her tea. 'Woman. Absolutely. I'd place a bet on it.'

Interesting, Nathan thought. So which of them was it that was trying to make contact with Alice Weston? The one who actually did the killing or the one that had tried and failed?

Evie might place a bet on the handwriting belonging to a woman. Nathan himself would put his money on the handwriting belonging to the killer.

* * *

The interviews with Fly, alias Felicity Connors, had begun at ten that morning. Sarah had taken a position beside her, the duty solicitor on the other side. Fly was more inclined to be cooperative this morning, now that she knew the old man had been arrested and that Lynn's flat been searched. But what about Lynn? Where was Lynn?

'It's only a matter of time before they find her,' Sarah reassured. 'In the meantime, you need to answer all the questions, make a statement, put this behind you as much as you possibly can. The only way you can move on, Fly my dear, is to tell the policemen all that you know so that they can stop any more killings. I know you don't want anybody else to die.'

DI Fox cleared his throat and looked sternly at Sarah. 'If you're quite finished, Ms Gordon.'

Sarah smiled sweetly at him and shot daggers with her eyes. She took Fly's hand and squeezed it. 'We're ready.'

DI Fox had a photograph of Lynn that had been taken from the CCTV camera at the home. There were several, but the clearest one he showed to Fly and asked her to confirm that this was Lynn Maxwell. He asked her next about Lynn Maxwell's family, about her friends, her social media.

'She didn't do social media. She didn't like it. I don't know her friends, I don't know anything about that.'

'Who else came to the flat? She must have had visitors?'

Fly shook her head. 'No one came. Lynn didn't like having people there. She went out if she wanted to see anybody. I never saw anybody come to the flat.'

'So if she went out when she wanted to see somebody, who did she go out to see?'

Fly shrugged. 'Never told me.'

'And you never asked?'

'Why should I? None of my business.'

'So how did she earn her money? That flat wasn't cheap, but she paid her rent six months in advance.'

'Never asked her. It was none of my business.'

'What about her regular habits — did she go out in the morning, come back in the evening? Was she usually out in the evening?'

Fly thought about it and then shrugged again. 'Sometimes she was there in the daytime when I was at school, sometimes she went out in the evening. When she went to see the old man, usually I went with her. Sometimes she went on her own.'

'But you never asked her anything?'

'Mam told me not to ask questions. She told me I should go and live with Lynn, that Lynn would look after me until I could look after myself. She told the old man, Mr Kane, that I should think of him like a grandfather. That I should do what he told me.'

'Even if that included killing people?'

'I never killed no one.'

'You tried.'

Fly shook her head. 'I don't think I tried very hard. I knew what he wanted me to do, I kept telling him I couldn't do it. Lynn said she'd do it for me, he wouldn't care as long as it was done. I told her he'd got a screw loose.'

'And what did she say to that?'

'She said she knew. Mam said I should go and live with Lynn, that's all I know. Lynn made sure I went to school, she made sure there was always food in the flat for me, she even said she'd take me clothes shopping, but I hate clothes shopping. She hugged me when I felt upset. She told me she would arrange Mam's funeral.' A look of great concern flashed across Fly's face. 'Who's going to do that now?'

'It will be sorted out,' Sarah told her.

DI Fox cast another angry glance in Sarah's direction, but he nodded and said as reassuringly he could manage,

'The funeral will be arranged, don't you worry about that. Now you need to tell us about Lynn. When did you start living with her?'

'Six months ago. When Mam became really ill. I thought I'd be able to go home again, but after about three months Mam said I'd have to stay. I'd been going backwards and forwards to Mam's house and to Lynn's, but then three months ago Mam got taken into hospital. They were going to transfer her to the hospice soon but she died anyway. So I moved all my stuff to Lynn's and I stayed there after that. She said I ought to try hard at school, and I did, but I hate school. No one likes me. They all think I'm weird.'

'Did you have friends at school before, before you moved in with Lynn?'

'At my old school. Before Mam became ill again. Before we moved back here. My old school wasn't too bad.'

'And where was your old school?'

'Mallingham. I went to Mallingham High School. I was scared in case Mam got sent to Mallingham General Hospital. I would find it hard to see her, but she ended up here so that was all right.'

'And you told me that Lynn's your half-sister. How do you know that?'

'Her dad and my dad are the same person, that usually means people are half-siblings.'

'And where is your father now?'

Fly shrugged. 'Don't know, don't care. He left when I was just little, and then when Mam got sick the first time, he never came home. I think it was then that she told the old man that he had to look after me, if anything happened to her. I think he might be related to my dad, but I don't know for sure.'

'You don't know much, do you?' DI Fox said.

'Mam said it was better not to know a lot of things. So I didn't. There were lots of things she didn't say. I think she didn't want them to be part of my life. It was just me and Mam, and she was kind, and I loved her very much and I still do. I didn't want to kill anyone.'

That strange distant look came back into Fly's eyes, the one Sarah had noticed before which seemed to indicate that she'd tuned the entire world out and gone elsewhere. Sarah knew instinctively that they'd get little more out of Fly that day, and she wondered how much more the girl knew anyway. She was clearly in shock from her mother's death, grieving and alone, and whatever else she might have done she was still just a kid. A kid that didn't ever seem to have much control over her situation.

'We found a computer in the flat — seems to have belonged to you. Did Lynn ever use it?'

Fly blinked and with effort pulled herself back from wherever she had gone to. 'I write essays on it, I submit stuff to school, we have to submit by email. Lynn didn't use it. I just kept it in my room.'

'Did Lynn have a computer?'

Fly looked confused and then shook her head. 'Smartphone. She just used a smartphone. She said she wasn't going to be writing any essays, so what did she need a computer for.'

'There were a number of pay-as-you-go phones found in the flat, what can you tell me about those?'

'They're phones you have to buy credit for,' she said. 'Lynn just used a smartphone.'

'So you never saw her use a pay-as-you-go?'

'Why should she? She had her smartphone. She paid for mine on the same contract. She paid for broadband and television, I think, with the same company. I think she paid everything by direct debit.'

'You don't know how she earned her money?'

Shake of the head this time. Fly slumped back in her chair and fiddled with a loose thread on her sleeve. She seemed exhausted, to have run out of what little energy she had. Fox asked more questions but got very little in terms of answers, and Sarah got the impression Fly couldn't even understand what he was asking questions for. She'd told them all she knew, and it *was* all she knew because she had refrained from asking questions. She had refrained from asking questions because her mother had told her that's what she must do. In this past year, Sarah suspected, the fact of her mother dying, slowly but surely, was probably the only thing that had really occupied Fly's mind or that she had cared about. The rest was just noise.

CHAPTER 32

Sarah left the police station around lunchtime when Ray came to pick her up. It had been a stressful morning.

'Nathan called,' Ray said, and he told her about the conclusions Nathan had reached about the cards that had been sent to Alice Weston.

'So it's possible Lynn sent them. Sounds a bit farfetched, but I suppose . . .'

'How did things go with Fly?'

'Not particularly well. She was a bit more forthcoming this morning, but the fact is she doesn't know much. I know it sounds ridiculous to say that she went through the motions of trying to attack Rose because some man she hardly knew told her to, but I think that's about what happened. It's not so much that she's not thinking straight, it's that she's not even thinking. I don't think she's stupid, she just seems to be operating by different rules.'

'She needs help,' Ray said. 'Clearly she's needed help for a long time now. Another little scrap that fell through the cracks — though don't forget, Sarah, she still threatened two vulnerable women. One of whom is now dead.'

'Fly didn't kill Erica Trimble, we know that.'

'And if she had told someone about Lynn, her death might have been avoided too.'

'I know you're right, Ray. I just feel sorry for her. She seems so lost.'

'I know. There are never any easy answers, are there?'

He glanced over at her, noting the strain around her eyes and the tightening of her mouth. Sarah should not have been dragged into this. He tried to change the subject, realising even as he spoke that he wasn't. Not really. 'Phil found something interesting — Rose and Lily knew Erica Trimble. They all performed on the same bill, by the looks of it, Lord knows how many years ago. He's produced a still for me to show to them, see if they recognise Erica from it, or anyone else for that matter. And Dave called — the fingerprints they took from the flat? Well, there's only Fly's and Lynn's in evidence, nothing even from random visitors.'

'Fly said they didn't have any visitors. She said if Lynn wanted to see anybody then she went out to see them. I don't think Fox believed her, but that's the way it seems to have been.'

'Well, certainly from the fingerprint evidence it does. No criminal record or anything else for Lynn, as yet. We still don't know who she is. The rent was paid in advance — by the same company that paid for Duncan Kane's care, which is interesting. They've got financial experts following that up. DNA might turn up some more direct links, of course.'

'And this Duncan Kane, do they know who he is yet?'

'Apparently not. Sarah, there's a little red car behind us, can you write its reg number down?'

Sarah delved into her bag for pen and paper and Ray recited the number. 'I wasn't certain before, but I think it's been following me. I've spotted it three times this morning.'

'Can you see who's driving?'

'Not clearly. A woman, I think.'

'Could it be her?'

'She's just turned off. I'm probably being oversensitive. I'll let Dave know anyway. You never can tell, can you?' He tried to sound casual but he couldn't fool Sarah.

'So when did you first notice the car?'

'Driving into town this morning. Then again when I went to see a client. Then again when I came to collect you. Enough times for it to be noticeable, not enough for me to be certain.'

'Oh really? You sound pretty sure to me. Ray, you shouldn't take any chances. This girl's already killed four times, that we know about.'

'Leave a message for Dave Beckett,' Ray told her. 'Just in case it's important. If there's an outside chance it's her then at least we know what she's driving.'

'You think she'll go after Rose again?'

Ray thought about it. 'Not yet. I think she'll wait for the fuss to die down and our guard to be lowered. But I don't think she'll just quietly disappear, not even now we've arrested Duncan Kane.'

* * *

Lynn was curious about the woman with Ray Flowers but guessed that it must be his partner, Sarah Gordon. She had done her research on the ex-detective as soon as he'd come into the picture.

Satisfied that they were now heading for home, she turned off and went to find some lunch and weigh her next move. The loss of the flat was annoying, but she'd left nothing there that felt important. The drugs weren't hers, a fact that might ultimately have consequences, but Lynn put that concern aside. First things first.

Fly she guessed was at the police station from which Ray had collected Sarah. The old man would be elsewhere. Mallingham, probably, as that was where he'd been arrested. She had a copy of his list and, more importantly, all of the intelligence she had gathered on the current locations of his chosen victims was still in her possession. She was, she felt, at least one step ahead of the police and in no immediate danger. Of that Lynn was certain. She had a job to complete and she wasn't about to give up now.

It was a funny thing, Lynn thought. When the old man had first told her what was on his mind she had thought he was joking. She'd entered into the speculation as a kind of intellectual exercise. It had been a bit of fun, wondering where these people were now, tracking them down, doing surveillance, creating scenarios. How could she get to them without being caught . . . The thrill of it captured her imagination and then actually doing it — well, that was something else.

She had watched them, stood with care workers when they took their cigarette breaks — asking for a light and then joining the conversation. Had studied delivery days and how they were organised. Had followed paper trails and plotted family trees. She had learned so much these past two years, she was pretty sure she could give the likes of Ray Flowers, in their fancy offices, a run for their money.

He'd had her practise everything first, telling her that preparation was the key. She had begun by breaking into random premises and watching strangers sleeping in their beds. Honing her skills, practising her craft, until she was not just competent but highly skilled. Which is why she'd had a lot more sympathy for Fly. Kane's preparation with Lynn had been thorough and careful, whereas with Fly it had been rushed and careless, as though he was getting impatient. Too impatient.

It was his fault really, that everything had fallen apart. He could have left Fly out of the picture and everything would have been fine. But no. He'd seen the opportunity to train yet another to follow in his footsteps, and arrogance, or something like it, had been his downfall. Lynn despised that. And then, she thought, he'd probably taught her all he could anyway. One thing she had to be grateful for, she supposed, that he had seen potential in her. He had understood what she was and accepted her, allowed her to grow into her new self. She had found her purpose in life.

She remembered the thrill of that first night when she'd broken into a bungalow, charged with bringing back a small souvenir, or with moving the furniture around and taking a photograph of what she'd done. Anything just to unsettle the owners of the house. It had been a laugh. A dozen such 'missions' had followed. He'd told her that Charles Manson had trained his Family that same way, sending them *creepy crawling*, as he'd called it. The old man seemed to like the idea of a connection with someone he regarded as a superstar. *Both just as nuts*, Lynn thought.

So what next, who was next on the list? It ought to be someone distant from here, there were police crawling all over the place. Sooner or later she'd have another go at Rose Spencer, and unlike Fly she would succeed. She didn't know what any of these people were supposed to have done — quite frankly, she didn't care. Lynn was having the time of her life and that was all there was to it.

* * *

The lunchtime news was full of half-cocked information, Ray thought. The flat being raided, an old man arrested from a retirement home, a young girl whose mother had just died and who was implicated in serious crimes. Perhaps murder. Perhaps the murder of those old people whose deaths had made so many headlines.

Listening to the lunchtime news and then reading through all of the available reports, Ray could see that they were fragmentary, confused, contradictory. But the press had the bit between its teeth now and if Fox or Beckett didn't hold a conference soon and explain something of what was going on, then the speculation would become wilder and more extreme by the time the six o'clock news played out on the television.

Someone, somewhere, however, must have made the connection between the break-in at Highbury House and the murders, because when Ray arrived there mid-afternoon a television crew and some local journalists had set up position just beyond the junction with the main road. Ray drove his car round the back of the building, glad that there were constables on hand to keep the media at bay.

173

Mrs Ellington was not pleased. 'I'm feeling a little under siege. Is there nothing that can be done about them?'

'As long as they're not coming onto your property uninvited, or causing a nuisance on the public road, then not a lot,' Ray told her. 'Think of them as added security.'

Mrs Ellington looked outraged but then had the grace to laugh. 'I suppose there is that. The ladies are in the lounge. Go on through.'

Ray was greeted with the usual enthusiasm and even more than the usual number of questions. He pre-empted them by handing Rose the image Phil had captured, explaining where it had come from. 'See,' he said, 'Erica Trimble, you and Lily, looking rather glamorous, I must say.'

'Oh, goodness, we were, weren't we? That's Erica Trimble? Lily, do you remember her now? Wasn't she the stand-in for the girl in that mentalist act, the one who ran off with a sailor?'

Lily thought about it. 'No, that was Netty somebody-or-other. Look at us both.'

'Can you remember where this might have been?' Ray asked. 'It looks as though it might have been a seaside venue, a theatre on a pier, maybe.'

'Oh, we did a lot of those in the early days. A nice, secure gig it was too, summer season.' She frowned. 'It could be any of a dozen places, Ray. It was all an awfully long time ago.'

'And you still don't recall anything about Erica Trimble?'

The twins exchanged a glance. 'Ray, we had a long career,' Rose said, 'and there were so many young girls we maybe knew for a few weeks before we all moved on. Girls disappeared from our lives all the time, they got married or got more secure jobs or they just realised the life was not for them.'

And Erica had been in the business for only a couple of years, Ray remembered. 'Is there anyone else in the picture who you do remember?' he asked.

Lily squinted at it. 'Now, the man in the back row, George something, he and his wife had performing poodles,

I think. And a rather vicious Yorkshire terrier that stole the show. He was on the circuit for years. They were all getting on even when we knew him.'

'This one here, I think he did some kind of comedy act, but I don't recall his name.'

'Anyone else?' Ray asked.

The sisters scanned the figures in the picture, dredging little details about one or other of those who gazed out from their shared past. A boat trip, picnics, late nights and dancing on days when the theatre was dark. Lily tapped the face of one young man in the second row. 'Now, what was he? Office staff, I think. Wasn't he an accounts person or something? Didn't he ask you out one night?'

Rose looked more closely. 'I believe you could be right. Terrible of me, but I don't even recall his name. Oh, but it was so long ago. But do you know what? I think this was Southend-on-Sea, we would have been eighteen or nineteen, certainly no more than that. Oh dear, where on earth do the years go?'

Ray left the photograph with them, promising that Phil had almost finished his transfers and, yes, they would all have a film night as soon as he had. He was slightly annoyed that he'd allowed himself to get his hopes up. The fact that Erica Trimble happened to be in the picture certainly didn't mean that they'd get lucky with the other victims. But he had, nevertheless, wondered — and yes, hoped — a bit too much.

* * *

Unknown to Ray, the image he had emailed across to Dave Beckett had caused a little more excitement at that end. Scanning the rows, looking for Erica Trimble, Beckett had found someone else. He was momentarily nonplussed that Ray had failed to make the connection and then realised that Ray would never have met or even seen a picture of Duncan Kane or whatever name he was going by back then. There he was, standing in the second row, looking at Erica Trimble or possibly past her. He had aged now, of course, but he was unmistakable. The shape of the chin, the shape of the nose, the general sense of the face.

Wondering if he was kidding himself, he asked a couple of colleagues and they confirmed what he was thinking. So, this man called Duncan Kane, Erica Trimble and Rose and Lily Spencer had all been in the same place, at the same time, God knows how many years ago. Were any others on the list in this picture too?

He didn't have time to call Ray at that point. The day was already going in unplanned directions. The initial interview with Duncan Kane had been delayed until late morning, five hours into custody time. Partly this was so that Kane could discuss his situation with his solicitor — and his solicitor had made a massive deal about this being an old man who'd had his sleep disturbed and therefore needed more time to prepare. Partly it had been because Beckett was waiting to see if any information came back that might identify this man before they embarked on the initial interview.

By eleven in the morning he felt he could put things off no longer. Fox sat in on this occasion, with Beckett leading the interview. The solicitor was definitely *not* a duty solicitor. He'd arrived in a lightweight summer suit with smart shoes and presented a heavily embossed business card. *Who paid for you?* Beckett had thought. He'd asked how the solicitor had been initially informed about his client's needs, and it turned out that the home had numbers that they could call should Mr Kane need anything. Anything at all, it seemed.

Interesting, Beckett had thought.

An hour into the interview they took a break, the solicitor once again citing Kane's age. It had been an unfulfilling hour, the solicitor taking a stern line and advising his client to offer no comment to whatever question might be asked. Beckett had expected no less.

They adjourned for lunch, Beckett feeling frustrated but knowing that this was going to go on for the long haul and that in the end their submission to the CPS would be on evidence found, not statements made. Then Ray's photograph arrived, and hot on its tail, fingerprint identification. Beckett scrolled through the list of aliases and known or suspected offences with a feeling akin to awe. Fox was looking over his shoulder. 'Well I'll be damned,' Fox said.

* * *

Ray's message to Beckett about the registration number of the little red car did not reach him until just before the interview was to be resumed. A note had been written and placed on his desk, but he had been so caught up in printing out and compiling the history of the man now known as Duncan Kane that it was a while before he got to it. There was an additional note that the number had been checked and did not belong to anything small, red or otherwise on four wheels. Beckett put out a general call for traffic to keep an eye open for the car. *She's taking a risk*, Beckett thought. The area was rife with ANPR systems. She would presumably be avoiding motorways and some of the major A roads, but even so, it was chancy. It suggested that she knew the area well, travelled by the back roads and had a good knowledge of the geography of the area. Or perhaps that she changed the number plate on the car at regular intervals, maybe even reverting to the genuine ones if she planned to travel any distance.

It was almost three o'clock in the afternoon when the interview was resumed.

Beckett pushed the photograph across the table for Kane and his solicitor to look at. 'You've aged well. It's an old photograph, but it's not difficult to pick you out.' He pointed with the tip of his pencil. 'Rose and Lily Spencer, Erica Trimble, you.'

Duncan Kane shrugged.

'And this is supposed to mean?' the solicitor asked.

'It's an interesting coincidence, I'm sure you'll agree.'

'What is an interesting coincidence? That my client happens to be in an old photograph? I'm sure that can be said of all of us.'

'True enough,' Beckett said. 'It appears your client has changed his name — on several occasions, as it happens.' Beckett flicked through the pages he had brought in with him. 'GBH, manslaughter, armed robbery, a half-dozen aliases. I could go on.'

'A man can change his name and make a fresh start. There's nothing illegal in that,' the solicitor said.

'So we are expected to believe that you're now a reformed character?'

'My client is an old man. His family organised his care but had no wish for past associations or mistakes to come back to haunt Mr Kane. His name change is legal and above board, and I have the paperwork for it should you wish to see.'

Beckett smiled. He was sure it was. None of this was particularly unexpected. He produced the list of victims. He had shown this to Kane and his solicitor earlier, but it had of course elicited no comment. 'Do you have anything to add about this list?'

He waited.

'Several people on this list have been victims of murder. Tarot cards were left that, so I'm told, relate to certain characteristics of those who have died. I'm told they are called significator cards.'

For the first time, there was a reaction from Kane. A flicker of annoyance crossing his face.

'We found a tarot pack in your room, Mr Kane. Do you read the cards, then? I expect that might make you popular with your fellow residents. You any good at it? I'm told it's quite a skill, interpreting all the meanings. There are, what, seventy-eight cards in total in a tarot pack?'

'It isn't a tarot pack. It's far better than that.'

Kane's solicitor looked at him in surprise. 'Mr Kane, I advise—'

'Not a tarot pack,' Beckett interrupted. 'I understood it was. I know it has a different name, Book of Angels — in fact, I spoke to the creator about it. Alice Weston is a very nice lady. She's quite horrified at the use that her cards have been put to.'

'She doesn't know what she's created,' Kane said. 'She just drew what she thought were pretty pictures, she has no idea what power she invoked.'

'And you do. Perhaps you'd like to tell me about it.'

Kane leaned across the table. 'If you're interested, buy a pack. There's a nice little book that comes with it, gives you all the meanings. Why should I do your work for you?'

After that it was back to 'No comment' again. There was another flicker of annoyance when Beckett showed him Lynn's picture, captured from the CCTV. 'The people at the home think this is one of your granddaughters, but I don't think she's related in the least. And as for this one' — Fly's picture this time — 'they think the same about her. And apparently the girls are half-sisters, or so they both believe. Of course, DNA will prove or disprove the connection, both between them and to you. So who are they? What have you done to them to turn them into killers?'

But Duncan Kane had said all he was going to say. The next hour Beckett spent effectively talking to himself, speculating and reading from the fact folder of past misdemeanours. Occasionally Kane looked amused, the solicitor annoyed, but that was about it. By the time the next break came Beckett was quite prepared for the fact that he would have to submit his case to the CPS on the evidence he had already gathered. He would have liked more, but he thought it would be enough to meet the threshold and at least keep Kane in custody, despite his age.

'We should lock him up and throw away the key,' Fox said. 'You know how many murders he's *not* been charged for?'

Beckett nodded. He could count too. Most of them were represented in the cuttings that Kane had kept in his room, what he referred to as his memories.

CHAPTER 33

Everything, Ray thought, felt flat. He sat at home with Sarah that evening, knowing that Beckett would still be interviewing Duncan Kane, Fly had been moved to more suitable accommodation in a youth detention centre some miles away and Rose and Lily would probably still be wallowing in nostalgia. He felt grumpy and useless and unable to settle to anything.

'Surely there's something you can do in the garden,' Sarah said. She'd watched him flick through every TV channel for the third time and get up to pace the room once more. 'Dave Beckett will be in touch once he has something to tell you. He's doing his best to keep you involved, you know that.'

'Not the same as being there.'

'No, of course it's not. But you aren't a policeman now.'

'I know that.' He had snapped at her, he realised. He'd not meant to do that.

Sarah raised an eyebrow, but she knew him too well to take his bad mood personally. 'It's not enough for you, is it? Flowers-Mahoney. The security company seemed like a good idea, and it was at the time. No doubt about that. But it's not enough, is it?'

He flopped down next to her on the sofa and closed his eyes. 'No,' he admitted. 'It's not. I'm bored, Sarah. That's the truth of it. But there's no going back to my old job now, is there?'

She smiled at him. 'Given that you left under a bit of a cloud, probably not. But there must be some way of using your skills. Of doing the same job in a different way.'

'I could buy a trench coat and a fedora, and become a private eye, I suppose.'

'You could,' she agreed, and poked gently at his comfortable waistline. 'I'm not so sure about the trench coat, though. Maybe something a little more forgiving?'

Ray opened his eyes and tried to glare at her. Sarah just laughed. She picked up the TV remote and switched the television back on. 'Let's see if there's anything different on the news now, shall we?'

She channel-hopped until she found a rolling news channel and they waited through the bombings and the civil unrest, the fraud and theft, and finally came to the news conference Beckett had apparently headed just an hour before.

Beckett summarised the tragic murders of Cora Hudson, Bethany Himes, Erica Trimble and Richard Hennessey. He confirmed that arrests in connection to the deaths had been made but was prepared to give no more details.

'However,' he said, 'we do ask the public's help with a related matter. We are trying to locate this young woman.' A picture of a blonde girl, clearly snatched from grainy CCTV footage, came on the screen. 'Her name is Lynn Maxwell, she's about twenty years of age and is being sought as a witness in relation to these tragic events. We believe she is driving a small red hatchback and that the registration number is something like . . .'

'Oh, my goodness.' Sarah stared at the picture on the screen. 'Is that what she looks like, this Lynn? She's nothing like Fly. And Ray, why doesn't he give out the full registration number? We made sure he had it.'

'I'm guessing they don't want other small red cars being driven by young blonde women to be discounted,' he said. 'I'm also guessing she's been driving on false plates.'

'He's going to be inundated with calls.'

'I imagine so.' It was, Ray thought, an unexpected move on Beckett's part. To make such a precise public statement at this stage.

'Why just as a witness?'

'Innocent until proven guilty,' Ray said. 'She's been charged with nothing yet. He's keeping his options open.'

'She'll go to ground. Surely. They'll never find her.'

'We don't know if she's got anywhere to go. We don't know her link to Duncan Kane. They'll be getting reports from all over.'

'Won't that muddy the waters?'

'Dave must think that's a chance he has to take. He must think she's ready to kill again.'

CHAPTER 34

Lynn was miles away. She'd heard the press conference on the radio and had been momentarily annoyed and then mildly amused. She'd reached the same conclusion that Ray had, that DI Beckett would soon have his hands full of false reports, and she was certainly not going to slow things down because some idiot police officer had released her name. What was a name anyway, but something to wear for a while. Her mentor had certainly worn out quite a few of them over the years.

She wondered briefly what was happening to him and Fly. She found that she was a little more concerned about her baby sister than she was about the old man. He was a means to an end, but she actually liked Fly, felt sorry for her, felt sympathy for a child that was as lost as she had been at that age.

The satnav told her to turn right at the next island, so she slowed a little in preparation. It was the most beautiful evening, the daytime blue darkening to night, and Lynn felt at peace with the world.

* * *

It was a couple of hours after the press conference when Ray finally got through to Dave Beckett. His friend sounded exhausted, Ray thought.

'Any progress?'

'A lot of blonde girls drive red cars. We're still no closer to knowing who she is, but it's a different story with Duncan Kane. According to his solicitor he changed his name because he's now a reformed character, and his family didn't want his past interfering with what's left of his future. He's had a fair few names through the years, but he was born Brian Anderton. He seems to have lost that name when he was in his early twenties, and he's been George Bannister, George Bain, and — here's one you're going to recognise — George Underwood.'

'Armed robbery, killed a security guard and one of the bank staff, threatened three more. Shot one of his own men for objecting to the way he was handling the show. That him?'

'That's the one. He was also the suspect in half a dozen murders, but nothing stuck. Two other people went to prison for offences we're pretty sure he committed. One died in jail and one was released on appeal. New evidence that he'd been somewhere else at the time.'

'And he ends up in an old folks' home in Mallingham. What are the odds?'

'Even ageing murderers have to end up somewhere. Of course he's denying the murder angle apart from the bank job, and he went down for manslaughter for that. Said at the time that he got in a panic and shot in their general direction. Witnesses who said otherwise were intimidated. His defence was that he was scared and lashed out. With a shotgun. Twice. Three times, if you count his own associate.'

'So who has been paying for his posh accommodation all these years?'

'A trust fund set up for him by a dead relative, apparently. Yes, I know, Ray, but my concern at the moment is getting hold of Lynn Maxwell or whatever her real name is. By the way, you won't have realised, but our Duncan Kane was in that picture you sent to me. Second row, three from the right. He's two along from Erica Trimble. Your ladies are in the front.'

184

Ray looked at his own copy of the photograph. 'Rose said she thinks he asked her out. That he was some kind of accounts bod in the theatre office. She didn't even remember his name. Do you think he's holding a grudge from way back then?'

'We've had a quiet word with what's left of his family. They were big players back in the day, as you know. There aren't many of the old generation left, but the message is Duncan Kane, as he is now, was becoming a bit of a handful even for them. Always making accusations, always causing trouble. They suspected that he might be losing whatever marbles he originally had.'

'Alzheimer's?'

'No, nothing like that. More that he was losing his hold on what was acceptable, even within that family. He's an old man, they felt an obligation, so they found a nice place for him to be. Changed his name, lost his previous identity, made sure he was well looked after, and by all accounts he seems to have settled down. But I suspect the alternative was six feet under, rather than a nice retirement.'

'Fly said when she visited him as a little girl that he was like a king or something.'

'Back then he probably was,' Beckett agreed. 'Ray, the fact that this girl Lynn seems to have followed you — I don't like that at all. If you or Sarah feel the need for some extra protection . . .'

'I don't think we're on her list,' Ray said. 'But thank you anyway. I am a little worried about Alice Weston though. If Nathan is right and Lynn Maxwell has been making contact with Alice, does that mean that Alice is under threat?'

'It's crossed my mind. We did a handwriting comparison, and the handwriting is definitely not Kane's or the younger sister's. But even disguised, it's a good match for Lynn Maxwell. I went back over the previous cards that Alice had kept, and from the dates on the postmarks she seems to send her cards after she's done something she's proud of. One was sent after Cora Hudson's death and one was after Erica Trimble's. She seems to be including Alice Weston in her narrative, whatever that narrative is. I'm glad she's not at home. Hopefully nobody will go looking for her at the Riverses'.'

'And the others on the list? Any progress on finding them?'

'Working on it,' Beckett said. 'The boss is considering putting out a public appeal, but that's a risky strategy. These people are getting on in years — should we warn them about a murderer, we might have them dying of a heart attack. But the other side of this is, there is no quick way of tracking any of them down.'

Telling Beckett that he would make sure John and Maggie kept an eye on Alice and reported any strangers that might come to the house, or anything else that might worry them, Ray rang off.

CHAPTER 35

Lynn had chosen her next victim carefully. This one still lived alone. He was independent, though he looked to Lynn to be frail. He had meals delivered once a fortnight that he stored in his freezer and reheated in his microwave. Other groceries arrived monthly from a local supermarket. He still liked to potter in his garden and spoke to his grandchildren and great-grandchildren at least twice a week.

She knew all this because she had done her homework. Erica Trimble happened to still be in touch with Arthur McAllister. Erica had been married to Arthur's oldest friend. Lynn liked the symmetry of this, she liked the connection.

Arthur lived in a little house at the end of a row, on the edge of a village. His garden wrapped around three sides, and although he could no longer manage it to the level he would have liked, he was still productive. He took the view that he should do a little bit every day. That he needed to keep fit and could keep on top of basic tasks twenty minutes at a time. The garden backed onto fields, and a narrow road that led to the village was just a few steps from his front gate.

His neighbours were good friends and he spent many an evening watching television with them, having a beer, setting the world to rights. Two evenings a week, he went with his neighbours to the local pub in the village. Together, they made up a not-very-successful pub quiz team, enjoying themselves immensely even though they never won. And most Friday nights found them in the bar, playing darts. Arthur wasn't bad at darts — at any rate, he was better at that than he was in the pub quiz.

Life on the little street at the edge of the little village was peaceful. The row of houses was inhabited mostly by retired people, with two young families at the other end. There was hardly any crime in the area and Lynn was quite content to believe that Arthur was easy target. He was old, what could he do?

But Arthur listened to the news and Arthur had recently lost an old and valued friend in Erica Trimble. A lady he had admired for the way she had looked after her own family and particularly taken care of the difficult man that her husband had become in later years.

He had also known Richard Hennessy, when they were all young. Knowing one victim of murder was bad enough, but to know two — well, it made him wary. Since Lynn had last surveyed the cottage, Arthur had installed security lights, not just at the back of the house but also at the end of the garden. The young couple at the other end of the row had also helped him put up a security camera that he could monitor from the house. Arthur McAllister did love his computer. So far it had only recorded foxes and badgers, but that in itself made interesting viewing.

Lynn, approaching the cottage from across the fields, had certainly not been prepared for the sudden illumination. Neither had she been prepared for the confident shout of 'Who the devil's there? I'll have you know I have a shotgun, and I'm not afraid to use it.'

This was not supposed to happen.

She shifted out of the light, heading towards the corner of the field.

'What is it, Arthur?' Another voice now. Lights coming on further down the row of houses.

'Step into the light where I can see you,' Arthur shouted again. 'I tell you, I have a shotgun and I'm not afraid to use it.'

What the hell! Lynn thought. But what could she do? What possible reason could she give for traipsing across a field in the middle of the night? Furious now, and clinging close to the hedge, she retraced her steps. She heard a gate opening, she heard people's voices and she was suddenly aware that there were others in the field and that people were actively looking for her.

Lynn broke into a run, sensed others running too, and then heard voices shouting at her to stop. She reached her car and drove off, just as three figures broke through the field gate and onto the road.

'Fuck, fuck, fuck. What the hell?'

It was the first time in Lynn's life that anyone had ever fought back and she didn't like it. She didn't like it at all.

CHAPTER 36

Duncan Kane was charged as an accessory to murder at eight o'clock that morning. Beckett got the impression that he was bored with the entire process. He leaned back in his chair, tapping his fingers on the table and occasionally glancing at his solicitor.

'You understand the charges, Mr Kane?'

'You think I'm stupid?'

'I have no opinion on that, I just have to ask the question. Do you understand the charges?'

Kane simply shrugged.

Beckett started to get up as though to leave and then paused. 'There's one piece of news that might interest you.' He took from the folder he was holding an image, a young woman blinking into bright lights, her face washed-out and pale, blonde hair almost like a halo around her head. Lynn, caught in the security light, a screen grab from Albert McAllister's laptop.

'She went after someone else on your list last night, a man by the name of Albert McAllister. He was apparently a friend of Erica Trimble's and her husband. I'm presuming you remember him, seeing as you wrote his name on your list. You designated him "King of Staves."'

Beckett caught the twitch of a smile at the corner of Kane's mouth.

'She was caught on security camera, which I'm sure you'll agree was careless. It seems, perhaps, she's missing your guidance.'

Kane's solicitor half opened his mouth to object, but Kane was there ahead of him. It seemed he'd given up all pretence now, that he had decided this pretence no longer mattered. 'What did you call her, *my protégée*? Well, I suppose she is.'

Beckett almost held his breath, not wanting to break the moment. He sensed Fox trying to catch his eye. 'Did you send her? Did you tell her that he was next on the list?'

'She's making her own decisions now. You won't stop her, you know, I taught her too well.'

'Mr Kane, I would advise you to make no comment, you really need to—'

'Oh be quiet, man, credit where credit's due. Yes, I trained the girl, I told her what to do and you've got to admit, she's done a good job so far.'

'Hmm.' Beckett took back the photograph and tucked it inside his folder. He paused, holding Kane's gaze. 'Albert McAllister is still alive and kicking. That photograph was taken when Lynn approached his cottage. Unknown to her, Mr McAllister had recently had motion sensors and security lights installed. And a CCTV camera linked to a laptop inside his house. He saw her coming. He and about a dozen of his neighbours chased her back across a field. Unfortunately, she made it to her car before they caught her, but she made a mistake, Mr Kane. A big mistake. Albert McAllister is still very much alive.'

If Beckett had hoped for this to worry Kane, then he was disappointed. Kane smiled. 'But there are others still on the list, Inspector. Just because she was unlucky once, doesn't mean she'll give up and, mark me, you still have no idea where these other people are. We both know that.'

He turned to his solicitor. 'Are we finished now? I've had enough of these people and I want a cup of tea.'

* * *

'Well, you got something,' Fox said a few minutes later in Beckett's office. 'Closest thing to a confession without actually getting a confession.'

Beckett nodded. 'He's right though, isn't he? There are still four people on that list whose whereabouts are a complete mystery to us. And he's right about the other thing. She won't give up. We have to try and guess who she's going to choose next, and we have to try and reach them before she does.'

CHAPTER 37

Fly lay on her bunk and stared at the ceiling. She was alarmed at how calm she felt, if that made any sense. But that was exactly how she felt. She was just profoundly relieved to be away from everyone. She was currently being kept in semi-isolation, allowed out for recreation and integration a few hours a day, but under supervision. The other girls in the unit scared her, but she had realised quite quickly that they did not scare her as much as Lynn or the old man had. She had liked Lynn in a way. Lynn was the one touchstone she'd had to normality. Lynn, who'd organised her life, woke her up in the morning, made breakfast some days or left a note to remind Fly to do it herself. Had her homework timetable and her daily schedule fixed to the fridge. Had behaved almost like a surrogate parent.

Now she had come to realise that Lynn was also someone she was afraid of, she had just not given herself time to think about it, hadn't opened herself up enough. Separated from these two, Fly could think only of the grief she felt at losing her mother. The space Lynn and the old man had taken up in her mind, in her day, in her emotions, was no longer there. It was just grief now and relief at being out of it all. Whatever the future brought, it had to be better than the past.

A solicitor had come to see her, but she hadn't really taken in what he'd had to say. She had gathered that Duncan Kane had been charged with something, and she had asked about Lynn and been told that he had no idea where she was. He had seemed reluctant to answer this question, which made her think he knew a lot about what was going on but was just not going to tell her.

She'd asked about her mother's funeral. Would she be allowed to be there?

He had smiled kindly at her and she'd got the feeling that he was relieved to have a question that he actually could answer honestly. 'Almost certainly,' he said. 'Nothing will happen in a hurry, not even your mum's funeral. But don't worry, it will be taken care of.'

She tried not to think about where her mother was now. She imagined that mortuaries were cold places full of tiles or stainless steel and she did not want to think of her mother there. Instead she remembered what it was like being with her mother when she was just a little girl and her mother had taken a picnic and a transistor radio up onto the castle mound and they had dance together with not a care in the world. Though even that memory was tainted now, as Fly realised just how many cares her mother must really have had.

* * *

Beckett called Ray to give him an update. Ray had seen the news item — it had made the national broadcast — on Albert McAllister and had made the immediate connection.

'So that *was* her then?'

'It was indeed. Foiled by an old man pretending to have a shotgun. And a bunch of neighbours.'

'So what will she do now? I don't suppose Duncan Kane has given you any idea?'

'Kane reckons she's now doing her own thing, making her own decisions. But he's practically admitted that he's behind all of this, so I suppose that's progress.'

'And are you any further forward tracing the other potential victims?'

'We've had a lot of people contacting us, and of course we're having to follow everything up with the help of local forces, with no way of knowing if the Richard Wilde found half an hour ago is *the* Richard Wilde, or the Marjorie Compton is *the* Marjorie Compton. Ray, that photo you sent me, I'm presuming it came from Rose and Lily Spencer.'

'It did. Phil's digitising some film for them. I gave him that photo of Erica Trimble riding the elephant and asked him to keep an eye open. What are you thinking?'

'I'm thinking it's quite possible that some of our victims are gone already — they'd be pretty old by now. If there was any way of cross-referencing the names we have with images from the film, or any photos that the Spencer twins might be in possession of . . . there's a chance it might get us a little further forward.'

'I already called Rose and Lily. They thought they recognised one of the names — Bridget Carr — but they don't think they have any pictures of her. I could get Phil to look for anything else with Duncan Kane, at least he's a fixed point.'

'OK, we'll start with that. Thanks, Ray. In the meantime we have enough phone lines to run a telethon, fielding calls from the anxious elderly and their relatives. It's going to be another long day, and I'm not sure we've made the right decision here.'

'I'm not sure there was another decision you could have made,' Ray said. 'If you hadn't released the names, and another person had been murdered, you can imagine what the press would have to say — and quite rightly.'

'But it's just as likely that the people we're looking for get lost in the noise, that we protect the wrong people, that she knows more than we do.'

* * *

The roar of Nathan's motorbike unsettled the quiet atmosphere at the vicarage. The children, recognising it at once, ran to the front door to let him in.

'He must know we've made a cake,' Maggie said.

Alice Weston sat on the stairs, watching as Maggie's children grabbed Nathan's hands and brought him inside. She had yet to see the young man crack a smile, but she got the impression that he really liked being around the Rivers family and that they were very fond of him. The kids especially. What, Alice wondered idly, would it be like to have kids, family? It was probably a bit late now and it wasn't something she'd ever particularly wanted, but she did wonder if she would ever regret that decision. Overall, she thought not, but the warmth of the Rivers family had been very pleasant these last few days.

She also acknowledged that she'd been slightly disappointed that Dave Beckett had not been in touch with her, beyond the brief courtesy call to check that she was still all right and didn't need anything. She had his number though, and Maggie had assured her that Dave liked her. Alice had plans to ring him when this was all over. *If* this was ever all over.

'It's lovely to see you, but what brings you here? And I have a Ladies' Guild meeting in about an hour. You might want to make yourself scarce before that or before you know it you'll be volunteering for the late-summer fête.'

'I've come to talk to Alice. Ray says that woman, Lynn, she definitely sent those cards. She's definitely been trying to communicate with Alice.'

'Why would she do that?' Alice asked.

'I think she wants your approval.'

'Approval? What on earth makes her think I'd approve?'

'I think maybe you should talk to Dave Beckett, tell him that you want to make a statement, an appeal for her to come and give herself up.'

Alice stared at him, momentarily stunned by the suggestion. 'What makes you think the police would even listen to me? Or that she would? Nathan, I don't want anything to do with this, it's been bad enough as it is. Just because some stupid woman or some vicious old man has decided to murder people, and leave my cards behind, that doesn't mean—'

'I think she might come looking for you anyway,' he said.

Nathan shuffled uneasily in the hallway, the children looking between the adults and wondering what was going on. They knew about the murders of course. Maggie and John sheltered them, but they also believed in being truthful and thought it was far better for news to be interpreted than for the children to go burrowing around trying to find things out on their own.

'Why? I only painted the damned things. Why should she be interested in me?'

'We know she is and I think she will. I think you should talk to Dave Beckett.'

'But if I made a public declaration of some kind, surely that would put me in more danger, not less.'

Nathan thought about it. 'I don't know,' he admitted. 'But it might stop her going after somebody else, and we can protect *you*.'

'Nathan, I don't think it's as simple as that,' Maggie said. 'Dave Beckett asked us if we wanted police protection here, but we felt it would draw more attention than it would solve anything. Do you really think Alice is in immediate danger?'

'The killer's not able to get to all the people on the list — she'll be angry now. She'll want to strike at somebody else. I think Alice may be a target.'

'Then I should leave here,' Alice said. 'No, Maggie, don't argue, you and John and the kids have been great, but what if someone has seen me here? You know how villages gossip, especially about their vicars. I wouldn't want to bring trouble to your door, and I certainly don't want to bring danger to it.'

'I brought a spare helmet,' Nathan said. 'You can come to the cottage.'

'And how is that going to be safer?' Maggie objected.

'It's in the middle of the village, and there's Evie Padget,' Nathan told her.

'Which is a sure-fire method of letting everybody in the area know that Alice is with you.'

'I know,' Nathan told her. 'But if Evie tells everybody that Alice needs looking after, then no one will move in the village without somebody knowing about it.'

'I'm sorry, but I think it's a crazy idea,' Maggie said. 'Alice, just phone Dave Beckett, see what else he can sort out.'

'No, Nathan is right, if she can't get the target she's chosen then she might come after me. I shouldn't be here, I won't endanger you or the kids. I'll go with Nathan. We'll tell Dave what's going on, but I think it's best if I go now.' She wasn't sure what lent the moment such a sense of urgency, whether she was catching something subliminal from Nathan, but the urge to leave was strong. 'And tell Dave that you want protection, that you're feeling threatened. This woman is dangerous. I don't want you to take any chances, Maggie. You don't know what she might do.'

Ten minutes later she was packed and ready to leave, and Maggie was on the phone trying to reach Dave Beckett and explain what was going on. She was alarmed to discover that someone matching Lynn Maxwell's description had been spotted at the end of Alice's street only an hour before. On seeing the police presence, the woman had asked neighbours what was going on, seemed overly curious. Once she'd gone, the neighbour had remembered the pictures of the blonde girl that had appeared on the news. She couldn't be a hundred per cent certain — the CCTV picture from the retirement home was blurry and the one taken from Albert's laptop was unnaturally burnt out and pale — but Dave Beckett had been about to contact Maggie with his own concerns.

'Just in case,' he said, 'I think we need to organise something better, make sure you and your family are kept safe too. I'm not happy about her having gone with Nathan.'

Maggie was suddenly irritated with everyone. 'I don't know what you've got against him,' she snapped, 'but you're wrong. I would trust Nathan with my kids' lives, and there are not many people I'd say that about. He will look after Alice, but Dave,' she added, irritation suddenly fading and giving way to deep unease, 'I don't mind admitting I'm a bit scared.'

* * *

Frustration was getting to Lynn. Out of curiosity, she'd visited the place where Alice Weston lived. It had been on her mind that she would like to speak to this woman. She had entertained herself sending the cards, wondering what Alice would make of them, but now this amusement had hardened into something else. It had transmuted into slow-burning anger that if Alice hadn't created these cards, then the old man would not have gone off on one and pushed Lynn in a direction that really wasn't hers. Sure, she was grateful to him, but she'd got caught up in somebody else's programme of revenge, and she really ought to be acting on her own account.

What right had this woman to create something as potent as this, something it was very clear she didn't even understand? The old man said that she'd just painted pretty pictures and hadn't got a clue.

There had only been the one constable stationed in Alice's street, and he had been chatting to the locals as though he was now a familiar part of the community. Thinking about it, she realised that he was probably just that. A community support officer, rather than a proper policeman. But according to the neighbour, Alice Weston wasn't there anyway. Now where would the blasted woman have gone to?

Lacking anything else to do, she'd driven towards Highbury House and found a police presence and a media contingent there. Irritating. But not unexpected, considering. She could still go after the others on the list. She had the advantage of knowing where they were and it was pretty obvious the police did not, but the incident with Albert

McAllister stung. It had unsettled her more than she had first realised. Lynn accepted reluctantly that there had been a moment when she had actually been scared. That hadn't happened before and she didn't like it one bit.

She pulled into a side road, some distance from Highbury House, and cut the engine. It was a quiet, tree-lined street and she doubted there'd be many people home at this time of the day. She was quite profoundly tired, having had no sleep the previous night and having slept in her car the night before that. She could book into a hotel, she thought. But she knew she was too restless to sleep, wound up and too annoyed. She needed to do something to make up for the night before, for the failure.

She glanced through the list again, thinking about location and distance, and who was least likely to have contacted the police. She really wanted to get to Rose Spencer — Fly had really cocked that one up, and it would be good to put it right. The fact that Rose had been prepared, or rather that old woman who had hit Fly with the cricket bat, really rankled.

How had they known?

She was in no doubt that Ray Flowers, this ex-detective, had something to do with it, but what she couldn't figure out was how he had got wind of what was going on. He'd had no contact with Kane, she was certain of that. He certainly didn't know her, and she was willing to bet he hadn't known Fly. The kid didn't think about doing anything apart from visiting her mother and going to school. She wasn't in contact with anyone else. The only time she went out was when Lynn took her to see Duncan Kane. So how had Ray Flowers known?

Suddenly her anger had a focus. If it hadn't been for him then things would have gone smoothly. Rose Spencer would not have had any warning, and even if Fly had still messed it up, Lynn could have gone in there and sorted it. End of problem, same as with that Trimble woman.

The rage that had been building against Alice Weston suddenly found itself transferred. It was all Ray Flowers's fault. He had somehow found out what was going on, somehow known about Rose Spencer, somehow managed to warn her. It had all gone wrong because of him.

The old man would have read the cards at this point, to find out what to do next, but she had come to despise that kind of reliance on something external. Circumstances had proved that he was not that clever in the end. Not as clever as he thought he was. Lynn was not going to fall into that trap. She had to rely on herself, end of. And Ray or that woman of his would make as good a target as any.

* * *

Nathan and Alice Weston were sitting in the kitchen at Mathilda's cottage, the cards laid out between them.

'Do you actually believe in all of this?' Alice asked.

'It doesn't matter. He does. I expect she does too — on some level, anyway. He let the cards guide him, then he guided her.'

Alice shuddered.

'It isn't your fault,' Nathan said. 'We cannot be responsible for what other people make of our creations. We cannot be responsible for what other people try to make of us. We can only reject their actions and their explanations.'

'How did you become interested in all of this?' she asked him.

'I grew up in this kind of religious commune. Everyone believed in everything. They were constantly looking for signs and symbols and meaning, and sometimes there isn't any meaning.'

'That must have been difficult. But you don't believe any more, or did you ever?'

'Some things have meaning. But what is important is what people believe the meanings are, because that changes the way they behave. If they get in the habit of believing that everything is connected, then it's almost like the world around them starts to respond, and then meaningful connections *are* everywhere.' He shrugged. 'Or at least it looks as though there are. I suppose everything *is* interconnected anyway, but if you only see the elements that reinforce what you're thinking then it can all seem rather magical.'

'Do you believe in anything?'

'Do you?'

Alice considered for a moment. 'I'm not religious. I suppose what I feel is that we are part of something bigger, sort of connected.' She laughed. 'I'm not sure how that's different from what you've been saying. It's not religious, I'm not sure it's even spiritual, it's just like awareness . . . I don't think it's something I'm very good at putting into words.'

'I don't think that's a bad thing,' Nathan said. 'The only people who frighten me are those who are certain they are right and can explain everything and that any alternative is wrong. If they believe they are absolutely right, then everyone else must be wrong and so you can't argue with them. You can't get them to see anything else.'

'I can't imagine you being afraid of anything much.' Alice looked at the cards that he had laid out on the table. 'Does this give you any insight?'

'I'm not sure.' Nathan had used the two greeting cards that he had borrowed from Alice as significator cards, in place of anything chosen from the Book of Angels. Then he had laid the others around them, foot and head, past and future, and then a run of four cards to the right-hand side of this initial cross. 'The same cards come up over and over.'

'At the head is the Transforming Angel,' Alice mused. 'At the base, the Tower, so whatever this person is trying to do is being undermined. In the recent past, the Ten of Swords, so things going badly wrong. Would that be when she attacked that old man, or tried to?'

'It could be,' Nathan agreed.

'Then you have the Hanged Man, so she's having to stop and think and plan. Well, I suppose you would, wouldn't you? Then this row of cards, at the beginning you have the Knight of Swords. If you're right, that's her, picking up the pieces and starting again. A new journey. So she has a new target.'

'And the target would seem to be the Queen of Swords,' Nathan said. 'Ray said that Rose Spencer was the Queen of Swords.'

'But it's unlikely she would go for Rose, there must be police and reporters and a lot of security around the house now.'

Nathan surveyed the line of cards that he had laid. Knight of Swords, Queen of Swords, the Wheel of Change, the Fool. 'The Fool is new; I've not seen that turn up before. You kept that design very close to the tarot.'

'I like the traditional image. The young man on a tight-rope, carrying his dog and all his worldly possessions in a pack over his shoulder, it's a nice picture to draw. Especially as he's sort of just heading off into the distance, not a care in the world. Fools rush in and all that.'

'I think I know what she plans to do,' Nathan said. 'I think there is somewhere else we need to be.'

CHAPTER 38

Duncan Kane sat on his bunk and stared at the blank wall without seeing it. In his mind's eye he could see Lynn, and he wondered where she was going and what she was doing and who she would choose next. He knew the details of his list by heart. Bridget Carr, she had been such a pretty little thing. He'd thought for a little while that she might be the one, but she was far too flighty — quick to go somewhere else when he had run out of cash. They had both been young, of course, but that was no excuse for bad behaviour.

Erica Trimble, he had lost his job because of her. She'd realised that he'd been skimming the takings, just a little off the top. Not that it mattered, there were always other jobs, but she'd betrayed his trust. She didn't have to say anything, no one would have known. And that same summer there'd been Rose Spencer. He had asked her out, been nice about it too, offered to take her to dinner. She'd just smiled at him, shaking her head, and said she didn't think so. It was clear she'd thought he was beneath her, and what was she? A magician's assistant.

Richard Wilde, he'd been the man that Rose Spencer had preferred. She'd been all over him for a while, and then she'd dropped him like a hot brick. But that was women all over, take what they want and then go. He could no longer remember what Marjorie Compton had done, only that she had annoyed him. Sometimes the memory of the anger was far stronger than the memory of the incident.

He knew that he was going to prison, but the thought did not trouble him too much. It would not be the first time. And when his family had imprisoned him in that home, telling him that it was all for the best, he had known that he could not count on anyone. That they would all betray him. He was simply trading one prison for another. But his was a name that would hold sway inside. He would revert, forget being Duncan Kane and go back to being the man whose name had once struck fear into the hearts of others. He would regain his rightful place. That thought pleased him.

* * *

Lynn had followed Ray home one night, more out of curiosity than anything else. Who was this man who had been visiting Lily and Rose Spencer and generally getting in her way? When she had found out who he was, what work he was involved with and his past, it had intrigued her greatly.

Today, she had parked her car some distance from Ray's home and circled round, finding a public footpath that led across fields and brought her behind the cottage where Ray and Sarah Gordon lived. But she had made up her mind what to do — it had seemed so obvious that she had been annoyed with herself for not thinking of it before. Ray now topped her list, and Sarah came a close second just because any injury to Sarah would indirectly be an injury to Ray Flowers. In the end it had been such an easy decision to make.

The rear of the garden had a high wall, but trees growing close by made it easy to access. She dropped down into the garden behind a massive laurel bush and stood listening to the sound of birds, watching the cottage windows. Through the gap at the side of the house she could see the front drive. Ray's car was not there, but Sarah's was. Fair enough then,

Sarah it was. Fate had chosen. She laughed at that thought. The old man would have used the cards to make this choice, now simple chance had made it for her.

For some time Lynn stood and watched, silent and utterly still so that not even the birds were disturbed by her presence. She had no wish to be taken by surprise, the way she had with those security lights at the back of Albert McAllister's cottage. It was a very pretty garden, she thought. One day, she'd quite like to have a garden. Right now, she didn't even have a proper home, but that could be sorted out. She needed to get this frustration out of her system first, and then she would be free of obligations. The old man would no longer have any influence over her and she could go her own way, *find* her own way in the world without anyone else telling her what they thought she should be doing.

She saw Sarah come into the kitchen, open the back door, step outside and put something in the recycling bin. The day was warm and she left the back door open when she went back inside. *Nothing like making it easy*, Lynn thought. Sarah disappeared from view for a moment or two and Lynn waited. She spotted her in an upstairs room, opening what was presumably a wardrobe door and hanging a dress inside. Then, shortly after, she was back in the kitchen.

She watched as Sarah filled the kettle, took biscuits from the cupboard, switched on the radio. Orchestral music drifted out across the lawn. And then Lynn crossed the garden, entered the kitchen and stood just inside the back door.

Sarah stiffened as she heard a sound and then turned. Lynn was satisfied to see the shock in her eyes.

'Hello,' Lynn said. 'I take it you weren't expecting me. You should have been, you and the ex-detective idiot you live with, seeing as you've interfered so much in what I wanted to do. You got in my way. I don't like people getting in my way. So you're going to be very sorry about that.'

She had expected Sarah to say something. Before this, her victims had been asleep or otherwise unable to fight back because of age or infirmity. Until Albert McAllister, of

206

course, but he'd just got lucky. That would not be the case this time.

Lynn had visualised this younger woman behaving in a different way. She'd expected her to react, to shout or scream or run and she was almost disappointed that Sarah did none of those things. Sarah stood across the room, quite still and quite silent. The electric kettle clicked off. Then Lynn raised the knife she was holding, gripped it firmly and advanced on Sarah.

Why did the woman not react?

'Scared of me?'

'Not particularly.'

'Oh come on, I saw how pale you went when I came in.'

'You startled me.'

'Startled you! Woman, I've come to kill you.'

'That's what you think. But I'm not old, and I'm not slow, and I'm not asleep. So how are you going to cope with that?'

Lynn was furious now. She lunged forward, thrusting the knife.

But Sarah was quicker. She grabbed the kettle, hurled it at Lynn. Freshly boiled water spilled all over her arm. Lynn screamed, dropped the knife. The kettle crashed to the floor, Lynn still screaming.

When she looked up, Sarah was gone.

If Lynn had been angry before, it was nothing to what she was feeling now. She heard the front door slam, knew her target was now out in the street. Heard her shouting. Lynn's arm pulsed in agony. She cried out again, pain and frustration merging into one tight ball of fury.

Lynn staggered out of the kitchen, back across the garden. From the front of the house she could hear voices. Shouting. Cars skidding to a halt. A motorbike, loud and throaty, scattering the gravel of the front drive.

She was at the wall now, wondering if she could climb. There were no handy, low-branched trees on this side of the wall, and when she tried to ram her fingers between the crumbling mortar of the ancient brick and flint, renewed pain from her scalded fingers caused her to cry out again.

A man's voice. 'Give it up, Lynn. There's nowhere for you to go.'

She turned, a wounded creature at bay, and stared at the man. DI Beckett stood between two armed officers.

'I've called an ambulance for you. Give up now and we can get that arm sorted out.'

She looked beyond him to where Ray Flowers now stood with Sarah and two other officers, out on the road beyond the house. Behind them, a young man beside a motorbike. Close by, a police car. She guessed there would be others.

Could she make it over the wall? The pain in her arm had not diminished — if anything it felt worse, as though something was burrowing deeper beneath her scalded flesh, sending shards of hot pain almost to the bone. But the sight of Sarah inflamed her even more than the pain in her arm, overrode the common sense that insisted she had nowhere to go and no means of getting there.

Sarah Gordon had done this to her. She was going to pay.

Roaring her anger, folding it into a ball of pain, Lynn hurtled forward, determined to get to the woman who had wounded her so badly.

A man shouted.

The pain in her arm was shrieking now. Lynn dropped to the ground, prone and helpless, armed police standing over her. DI Beckett, stumbling back to his feet, released the hold he had on her injured arm.

Lynn was stunned. She had heard the shout and heard what she'd thought was a shot and had momentarily believed that she'd been hit. Instead, she realised, he had simply grabbed at her as she leaped forward. The pain in her arm had done the rest.

'Stay down.' One of the big men with big guns had spoken that time. DI Beckett stepped out of her line of sight.

The old man had not prepared her for this. She closed her eyes and let the tears flow.

* * *

Beckett walked back to the group standing out in the road.

Sarah lashed out at him. 'You took your bloody time.'

'I know. I'm sorry. We moved as fast as we could.'

She took a deep breath and nodded. 'I know.'

'You should have left the house the moment you spotted her.'

'And let her walk away, come back another time. Kill me or someone else?' She shook her head. 'I saw something out of the corner of my eye. So I went outside and put stuff in the bin. Then I was certain it was her, so I called for help. I thought if I could just keep her here until you came . . .'

She took a deep breath and Ray wrapped his arms tight around her. He seemed, Beckett thought, lost for words, unable to trust himself to speak.

'What's he doing here?' Beckett nodded in Nathan's direction.

'He warned me she might be coming,' Sarah said. 'That's why I was watching, why I even noticed her at all.'

'And how did he know?'

Sarah smiled. 'He said he saw it in the cards.'

EPILOGUE

There were more people at her mother's funeral than Fly could have imagined, even if they were mostly people she did not know. DI Beckett came over to her and explained who everyone was and what part they'd played in bringing this nightmare to an end. Sarah Gordon and Ray Flowers, Alice Weston and Nathan. And despite the fact that Fly did not know them from Adam, she was glad they were there. The small chapel still seemed empty. Perhaps the presence that surprised her most was the one she did recognise: Elspeth Moore, dressed in her accustomed tweeds and a large black hat.

Fly stood between two prison officers, silent as the small congregation sang hymns, and listened as a speaker who had never met her mother extolled her virtues. She was kind, the man said, she loved her daughter. She liked to dance and enjoyed music. There wasn't much more that anyone *could* have said, Fly thought.

As Fly was led out at the end of the service, Elspeth stepped forward and asked if she could have a word. Dave Beckett nodded that it was all right.

'Why did they all come?' Fly asked.

'Four people are dead and many more individuals have been damaged by this tragic business, including those who have come today,' Elspeth told her. 'But nevertheless they do not believe that your mother deserved to go to her grave unmourned and unattended. Now, my girl, I cannot forgive you for attacking my friend, but I do believe there were mitigating circumstances. So I wondered, perhaps you would like me to write to you and perhaps you would like to write to me. Letters, you know,' she added. 'Or emails if you prefer, assuming they allow you to do that from wherever you end up.'

Fly blinked in surprise. Sarah squeezed Ray's arm. 'Well I never,' she murmured.

'I'd like that,' Fly said. 'I'd like that very much.'

'Good, that's settled then. I expect either Ray or Inspector Beckett will provide me with details of where to send my missives. You know my address, don't you?' She smiled mischievously.

She stood watching as Fly was led away, and Ray came over to her. 'That was kind,' he said. 'Do Lily and Rose mind you doing that?'

'My dear Ray, I have not consulted them. Why should I? I do what I think best and what feels *just*, and I don't think that young woman has had a chance to start her life yet. I think perhaps I might be able to help her.'

Ray watched as she straightened her jacket, tilted her hat and marched off.

'Everybody needs an Elspeth Moore,' Sarah said.

'Fly could do worse than to learn from her,' Ray replied.

After the service they both left for their respective places of work, glad to be given the chance to do what was ordinary and normal. Ray sat in his captain's chair and stared out of the window. A proposal had been made a few days before that he thought he would take up. It was work he could do alongside the demands of Flowers-Mahoney, work he was well suited for. A cold case unit had been set up, of a rather specialised kind. Cases that had peculiarities, unsolved and shelved investigations, often murder, that had ritual or occult overtones. Cases that dealt with the murky, troubled world that most police officers would prefer to ignore. Ray understood that attitude. An armed robbery with a purely monetary motive was an easier thing to understand.

'The pay isn't good,' Dave Beckett told him. 'And it's likely to be a thankless task, but apparently there's a team being put together, ex-officers who have experience with the weird and the wonderful. I took the liberty of putting your name forward.'

The news had arrived that morning that he had been approved. Frankly, Ray couldn't see that many people would be volunteering for this kind of thing.

'At least you won't be bored,' Sarah had said.

Ray reached across his desk and pulled a stack of folders towards him. Everyday stuff, reviews on security systems they'd fitted over the past year, updates and servicing contracts. Ordinary and concrete and paying the bills. But not enough to satisfy his curiosity and his detective expertise. He felt more content to deal with them now that something else was on the horizon.

'The Chariot of Time,' Nathan had said when he had read the cards for Ray the night before. 'A new and exciting journey.'

Ray Flowers, ex-DI, certainly hoped so.

THE END

Thank you for reading this book.

If you enjoyed it please leave feedback on Amazon or Goodreads, and if there is anything we missed or you have a question about, then please get in touch. We appreciate you choosing our book.

Founded in 2014 in Shoreditch, London, we at Joffe Books pride ourselves on our history of innovative publishing. We were thrilled to be shortlisted for Independent Publisher of the Year at the British Book Awards.

www.joffebooks.com

We're very grateful to eagle-eyed readers who take the time to contact us. Please send any errors you find to corrections@joffebooks.com. We'll get them fixed ASAP.